The Refuge

Finding healing in a hurting world

by David P. Smith, M.D.

Copyright © 2004 by David P. Smith, M.D.

The Refuge
by David P. Smith, M.D.

Printed in the United States of America

ISBN 1-594676-72-0

All rights reserved solely by the author. The author guarantees all contents are original and do not infringe upon the legal rights of any other person or work. No part of this book may be reproduced in any form without the permission of the author. The views expressed in this book are not necessarily those of the publisher.

Unless otherwise indicated, Bible quotations are taken from The Wesley Bible. Copyright © 1990 by Thomas Nelson, Inc.

www.xulonpress.com

Acknowledgements

I don't think that I would have been able to have written this novel without the leadership of the Lord in my life. As Psalm 31 states, He is my Rock of refuge and my Fortress of defense. He has redeemed me, led me, guided me, and is my strength. My loving wife and best friend, Autumn, has always been and continues to be an inspiration and support to me; she's the most giving person that I know and I thank her for putting up with me during the time it took to write this. There were several other editors and critics that I depended upon to help, including my mother, Genny Wilkinson of Busy Corner community, MS; my father-in-law, Roger Davis of Monroe, NC; a special friend, Rev. Ed Sudduth of McComb, MS, where Ed is the senior adult minister at First Baptist Church in McComb; and Winston Boone of McComb, MS, a dear friend. There are many other people that I don't have the room to name here, but have supported me over many years. I thank every one of you who have kept me in your prayers and have been the Christian witness in your life that the world needs to see. Now, I thank those of you who will pray that this book will be a witness for Him and that He will use this book to lead many to come to know Him.

Foreword

You and I live in the midst of a hurting world. Hurting people are everywhere. As we traverse the day to day pathways that comprise our portion of the world, we meet them. They represent every race, every age group, and every socio-economic level. All of them have one thing in common: they are hurting. Out of quiet desperation, they are searching—-searching for someone to care, to understand, to love unconditionally, and someone to point the way to the answer.

Life is made up of relationships. Meaningful relationships, born out of one's relationship with Jesus Christ, help to form the fabric and fiber of who we are and who we become. In his book, "The Refuge," Dr. David P. Smith strikes the heart of the matter as he so graphically portrays the "true to life" experiences that are so prevalent in our society today.

David Smith is a committed physician who walks closely with the Great Physician. He is truly a "man after God's own heart." He has a passion for righteousness, and the greatest desire of his heart is to please the Lord in every aspect of his life. He loves people with the love of the Lord and seeks to minister to the deepest needs of the heart as he points them to the answer, Jesus Christ.

I commend this book to you. Read it with an open mind. It will minister to your heart and change your life. You, too, can become part of the answer.

—Rev. H. Edwin Sudduth
McComb, Mississippi

Preface

We live in a society today that has lost its moorings. People toss about on the sea of life with no anchor at all, or might have a tattered one that cannot hold when it's really needed. Even in the Christian community, so many are out there who don't understand that they have a refuge in Him, if they seek Him. Too often, there is a form of godliness, but no power. Christ is the same today as He has always been. He never changes, but He can change us if we let Him. Thank God.

This book is a novel. It doesn't reflect the life of any one person in particular, but the individual stories and events are drawn from the real experiences of the many people that I have encountered and know. It's about tragedies that are all too common in our society; this is the reality of our day. It's not just about the tragedies, although. Just as in life, there are mountain top experiences in the lives of characters of this book. There are then, just as in real life, the difficult valleys that come again. The Bible tells us that our Lord, after overcoming the enemy during the forty days in the wilderness, had the devil leave Him, but only for a season. We only become stronger as we choose to allow Him to completely control our lives; He gives us the power to overcome any struggle if we take refuge in Him.

A remedy that will heal our land is available for many of the ailments plaguing us all. That remedy is a true *relationship* with our Creator, not just knowledge, or acknowledgement, of Him, but a *relationship* with Him. It is possible to have the refuge that we all need to make it through life and be whole. It is possible to be healed of the hurts that haunt us when we let Him do the healing work that only He can do. Sometimes we need His precision, surgical hands to take out something that doesn't need to be there. Sometimes we just need to be held in His arms knowing that He really does care for us like His children. A God that knows the number of hairs on our heads, and even knows when a sparrow dies, is the same God that wants to be the first priority of all of our lives. We have to choose to let Him be in that place and when we do, we can have a peace that the world cannot comprehend, cannot know, and cannot take away.

I've met too many patients that don't understand these truths, and many other truths, that our Creator gave us in the Bible. Unfortunately, I've also talked with a few physicians who don't understand either. They treat their patients with the medications of the day, which are great and I'm glad that we have them, but there is a spirit in each of us that needs to be cared for also. The Bible tells us that we are to be our brother's keeper; ignoring the most important part of us and "leaving that to the pastor" is not an option for any Christian who really does care about other fellow humans. As studies have shown, the majority of patients want physicians to pray with them. I believe they really are also saying that they want a physician who truly does care about them. I'm glad that kind of physician is out there, all over God's creation. Human physicians aren't perfect, but the Great Physician is. Unashamedly, in His love, we must provide the directions to the road that leads to The Refuge.

Table of Contents

CHAPTER ONE

Encounter with Dr. Wesley

The lady walked in the office with a disheveled look; there was tenseness in her face and body posture. Years of worry and disappointment had marked her face with its inerasable lines. As she came up to the counter to check in, she wondered if anyone here would be able to help her, if anyone would understand. "Maybe I should just go back home," she thought just before she signed her name on the list to be seen.

The receptionist asked her to fill out some papers and return them when finished. She then went back to her chair to sit down. *"They just want to see what they can charge me,"* she thought when she was filling out the information. She reviewed the questions about her health and checked off problems she was having: "headaches, neck pain, muscle aches, chest pain, palpitations, shortness of breath, abdominal pain, diarrhea, constipation, and fatigue." She thought about some other things she wanted to write down, but hesitated. When she finished, she brought the paper work back to the receptionist and sat back down to wait. *"I wonder if I should have written that down,"* she thought again. After sitting for a little while, the nurse came to the door and called, "Mrs. Ashton?" Sarah timidly arose and followed the nurse to the back where she was weighed and her vital signs were checked.

"How are you feeling, today?" the nurse asked.

"Okay, I guess," she replied, knowing she didn't mean a bit of it. She went through some of her complaints with the nurse and was placed in a room to await the physician to come see her. She sat nervously and fidgeted while she waited, but the tension lessened as she sat there and had some time to think.

The exam room that she sat in was different than ones she had been in before and actually had a calming effect. Everything in the office, from the magazines in the waiting room to the pictures on the walls, was uplifting to her. Sarah said a quick prayer for Him to help her. All of her thoughts about why she shouldn't be there left, and she was glad now that she had overcome the battle playing out in her mind. After not too long, the door opened and in walked the physician.

"How are you today, Mrs. Ashton?" the physician, Dr. Tom Wesley asked.

Sarah thought for a split second, but then replied with the usual, "Okay, I guess."

"Sarah, I notice that you've checked off quite a number of worrisome complaints here. Can you tell me about them and we'll see if we can figure this out?" he inquired.

She then told him about her episodes of pain that she was having in her chest and in other areas. Her chest pain didn't sound like any type of heart condition and Tom could tell that she probably had irritable bowel syndrome bothering her. The more she talked, it was obvious to the good physician that there was much more going on here than was being relayed directly. As she talked, she could tell that Tom was listening to her intently. She thought to herself, "Could he maybe help me?" As she continued, he noticed a tear in the corner of her eye that was just starting to form; it got larger and then it flowed ever so slowly down her face that had begun to soften in its appearance.

"Sarah, what's really bothering you?" Dr. Wesley kindly asked as he leaned forward in his chair. He compassionately looked into her eyes that revealed the hurt on the inside longing to be seen. She weighed whether she should allow him to see what was hidden deep inside and whether he would even care about her anymore at all if he learned completely about her. She noticed his concern as she looked back into his eyes that revealed he truly wanted to help her.

The tears started flowing more freely. She sobbed almost uncontrollably, like a solid, iron gate which held in her emotions was pulled up and out of the way so she could express them freely. Through her tears and sobbing, she told of how she'd been suffering with these ailments, which really were conditions of the heart. It was not the physical heart in the center of the chest, but the heart among us that represents the soul and spirit of the person. Sarah's spirit had been crushed, and the only way she knew to express it was through the physical complaints that abounded within her.

She could tell that Dr. Wesley was genuinely concerned about her and that she would be safe to discuss with him the demons that tormented her mind and how they got there. "Dr. Wesley, I just don't know if I can talk about this. It's just, it's just so hard to talk about," she stammered out and quickly grabbed some nearby tissues to dry the fountain of a long time of withheld tears flowing from her eyes.

"Sarah, you don't have to worry. I'm here to help you, and you really can trust me; whatever you tell me stays between you and me," reassured Dr. Wesley. He thought to himself about the other patients he had to see and whether he really had enough time to listen to what sounded like it might be a time-consuming discussion, but quickly brushed the thought away as he realized what might be at stake here. She could be on the verge of suicide, or other horrible things that ran through the good doctor's mind. Dr. Wesley knew that he would never be able to deal with his conscience if something awful, which he could have prevented by just taking some time to listen, happened to this patient.

She held her face down and looked up with a look that reminded Dr. Wesley of the way a puppy looks when it's hurt. She was visibly ashamed about the whole matter, and, still looking for signs of acceptance and understanding in the doctor's face, hesitated as if she were counting the costs of full disclosure. "Would this be a place of refuge for me?" she thought.

Sarah, feeling more secure, began to delve into her past hoping to give Dr. Wesley an understanding about her present predicament. She started where it all began, her beginning, with her parents, Frank and Julia. Sarah had just moved into the area. She remembered a lot about her great-grandparents, grandparents, parents, and brother. She remembered some good things about them, and she also remembered some things that she wished she didn't. She realized how the actions of one can affect many, for good or for bad. She understood well how a split-second decision can have ramifications for generations. She also knew that for the cycle of hurt to stop, she had to be healed, but how could she? Who would ever be able to bring her to a point of being able to feel safe again, to have a normal relationship with others that she longed for so much, to have a family around that truly loved and cared for her and each other, and to have a real, true peace? Sarah would discover the answer to all these questions and more. Over the next several visits with Dr. Wesley she related to him the story that follows of how she got to where she is now.

CHAPTER TWO

Julia Meets Frank

Frank Dupree, her father, was only thirteen years old when he had to start working to make a living to help his parents. Times had been hard for them all due to the depression of the 1930's. He started out working in a local, Chicago grocery store sweeping the floors, putting up stock, and really just doing whatever they needed him to do. He was a hard worker and his employer really liked him because he put his all into his work. Frank didn't make a lot of money, but what he brought home to help the family made him proud that he was contributing to keep the bills paid. He didn't study as much as he should because he just didn't see the need for it at that time. By the time he was fifteen, he was getting more responsibility at the grocery store and was really enjoying himself. He had learned a lot about the world, and the ways of the world, during the time he had worked.

When Frank was little, his parents took him to church. They thought he should go, but they never attended too often themselves. "Frank can decide for himself if he wants to continue to go to church," was his father's philosophy.

Frank went for a few years intermittently, but as he got older he decided for himself to follow his parents' example of not going either.

Frank's job brought him some money, and some temptations came with it. With the moral influence in his life misguided, it wasn't long before Frank discovered one way of getting away from life's displeasures— alcohol. He would sneak a few drinks with some buddies he had met, trying to hide this activity from his boss who was good friends with his parents. When he turned sixteen years old, Frank had started making alcohol a more regular part of his life and included it in his routine weekend activities. Unfortunately, he also came into contact with another influence—pornography. His dad had a "girlie magazine" that Frank had found hidden under his parents' bed. It wasn't long before Frank and his friends decided to start experimenting with the objects of their fermenting desires. They learned about some women in the inner part of town who had no scruples about whom shared their beds.

In another part of town, the better side of town as some called it, Julia Miller lived in a very nice neighborhood and had a totally different type of life. Her father, Cecil, was an attorney and was well respected in the area. Julia went to an excellent school in the area and regularly went to church, most church activities, and was always accompanied by her dedicated parents who only wanted the best for her, and themselves.

As Julia got older, she started evaluating what she was taught. As most teenagers do, she questioned her parents and what they believed. There were some questions in Julia's mind about why her dad always talked so differently when he was at church than when he was at home or work. She wondered about some of the people for whom she saw him doing work; when Julia asked him about what seemed like a discrepancy between what he said and what he did, he told her "that was just business."

When Julia was fifteen years old, she and some of her friends went driving one weekend night and decided to stop at a local cafe to get something to eat and chat for a while. While they were sitting there talking, in walked Frank with some of his friends, and they sat over in the booth that was across the restaurant from Julia's booth.

"Hey Frank," whispered Don, one of Frank's buddies, "Look over there; she looks pretty good. I dare you to go over and ask her out."

Frank, not about to show his fear in any situation, jumped up and announced, "Well, I'll just do that. Watch how the master deals with the ladies." Frank tried to get his thoughts together and figure out what he was going to say, as he slowly slinked over to Julia's booth.

Julia and her friends noticed the stirrings in the booth over there and Julia, the shy one of the bunch, frantically asked Melissa, her best friend, "That guy looks like he's coming over here! He's looking at me. What do I do?"

Melissa told her in a hurry, "Just be yourself. Smile at him." Julia smiled as big as she could manage, but her smile was only a cover for a state of panic inside.

Frank, as confident as ever, boldly and softly spoke, "Hey, you're new here, huh?"

"Yeah, my friends and I were out driving and decided we would stop here and see what this place was like," Julia explained. She calmed down a little as she got out those first few words. "How long have you been coming here?"

Frank coolly looked into her soft, blue eyes and said, "Just long enough to be able to meet you. Could I take you out sometime?"

Julia was shocked that someone was asking her out on a date so soon. She knew she liked him, but she also knew that her father had said that she couldn't date anyone until she was sixteen. "I'll have to ask my parents. I might be able to meet you here with my friends later though."

After he got her telephone number, Frank told her that would be great and then strutted like a rooster back over to his booth. He had certainly impressed his friends. He could tell Julia was different than the other girls he had been seeing. Frank and Julia met there again the next week and, although Julia didn't ask her dad if she could date, they would go off together while the rest of their friends stayed at the cafe. Frank knew just all the right things to say to win over Julia's heart. As they got to know each other more, Frank started becoming more physically intimate with Julia and, although she resisted at first, she was afraid she'd lose him if she didn't go along. They eventually began to get too involved. After Julia started having some nausea each morning, she found out she was pregnant after visiting a nearby Crisis Pregnancy Center. Julia suspected that she was pregnant after talking to Melissa and went to the clinic alone one afternoon when her parents thought she was running other errands.

What was Julia going to do now? Her parents expected so much from her, and now she had let them down; she had let herself down. This was certainly a crisis for her and she knew that she had no choice, but to tell her parents the truth.

CHAPTER THREE

Life Gets Tough

Julia's parents were very upset after learning about her pregnancy. Her dad told her she'd just have to leave after he asked her why she "had to go and embarrass their family so much." Julia's grandparents, Elizabeth and William, were devastated over what had happened, too. Elizabeth did the only thing she knew would help—she prayed, and told Julia that she still loved her regardless.

Frank felt some sense of responsibility so he asked Julia if she would marry him. Frank's parents certainly could not afford to help him and they decided it would be best if he moved out to his own place. A very small apartment in the inner city was where they would call home. Frank would continue working at the grocery store, and Julia realized that she would soon have to help raise a child and contribute to the family if they were going to make it. They were two kids trying to start a household, without anything much to call their own, and a child was on the way.

Julia's young, innocent face changed into a much older appearance quickly. Gone was that carefree spirit in her walk, replaced instead with the shuffling of slow steps, as if she were carrying the weight of the world on her shoulders alone. She didn't know how she was going to be able to do this and didn't know to whom to turn. Her parents felt betrayed, but were more concerned about their reputation than how to help their daughter during the worst crisis of her life thus far. They had nothing to do with her, but didn't realize their own earlier betrayal of Julia when their values didn't coincide with their actions. Julia's dad wished now that he had spent more time with her, but his pride wouldn't let him admit it.

Frank decided to marry Julia because he felt that was what he had to do. Julia's parents were not happy at all about this latest development and would not give their support. Frank didn't have much money for their wedding, so they went to the local justice of the peace and were married two weeks after she discovered she was pregnant. The newly married couple quickly realized that there was more to marriage than they thought it would be. The apartment rent took a lot of Frank's money that he made at the grocery store, and his friends that he formerly hung around with were now doing other things without him now. Frank felt alone and was afraid. He treated Julia okay, but he also started relying upon that bottle of forgetfulness, alcohol, to help him feel better and take him to where he would not have to face reality. He wished he could go back and start over. He wished he could just get away. He wanted to be what he thought a husband and soon-to-be father should be, but he just couldn't handle the responsibility of it all. He felt like a failure and started spending less and less time at home, choosing instead to go out with his buddies again.

All of Frank's friends had problems of their own. There was Rick, who talked about his dad who had left when he was child. Rick and his mom had to make it on their own and didn't make it very well. Rick's mom was at work most of the time, even though she would rather have been at home with him. She knew that he was not getting the attention that he needed, but she had no choice. She relied upon others to help raise Rick, but didn't really know what they were teaching him. He learned a lot on his own, just like Frank did. Frank was his best friend, and they both taught each other about life. They saw some of life's worst and had come to expect the same of almost everyone.

One of Frank's other friends was Don. He was the leader of their group, not by any vote of any kind, but just because of his strong personality. When Don spoke, they all listened. He was a little older than Rick and Frank and had more experience in the world than they had. Don was the one who introduced them to alcohol. He got some beer out of his parents' refrigerator; there was so much in there that he knew his dad wouldn't miss it. And besides, his dad let him drink it with him some when Don was little. Don liked the attention he got when his dad and those older men would gather around and laugh at someone so little drinking beer. Frank and Rick didn't like the taste of it at first, but they drank it anyway and soon adapted to the taste of it. They all just wanted acceptance and this was one thing that made them feel older, feel together, and feel like they belonged at least to something.

The first time Frank got drunk, he felt terrible the next day. While he was drinking, however, he was carefree and didn't feel encumbered by all the problems that were occurring about him. It was like he could escape into this world far away where he felt in control, although he had no control. When Frank decided to marry Julia, he said that he was going to quit drinking. He had the best of intentions, but when the pressure started coming, Frank remembered how he felt when he used to go and drink with his friends.

Julia knew something was wrong with Frank, but didn't know which way to turn. She wanted to be able to turn to him, but he couldn't even handle himself. Especially with the baby on the way, she remembered especially the words Elizabeth, her grandmother, had said: "Julia, you've made a mistake, but the Lord can help you if you'll let Him. I'll be praying for you everyday." Although she remembered those words, she did so with a sense of disdain because of the way she saw her parents live. Julia heard them say often to others that they would pray for them, but she never saw them praying at home. They said they prayed for her, but she never saw them or heard them do so. They said the right things to the people at their church and Julia liked how her parents acted while they were at church. However, as soon as they were back home, things were back to usual. Julia had come to learn that her dad only looked at church as a way of getting business and looking good to the community.

Her mom, Susan, also went along with this facade that their family had no problems; she refused to see the problems before it was too late. When Julia ended up pregnant, Susan suggested something that even Julia knew was abominable. Her mom said quietly that they could go to a doctor that could help Julia "get rid of this problem." Julia felt pressured to give in to her mother's suggestion, but she knew in her heart that this was just wrong. Her mom had told her that no one would have to know because her dad had a friend that would "help them." It seemed to Julia that her parents cared more about what the people at church and in their circle of friends would think, rather than actually caring about her. This was the way it had always been, she thought.

Without much support from her parents and realizing her new husband was losing interest quickly, Julia knew she was on her own. She felt so alone. Their little apartment was so small compared to where she had grown up and the life she was accustomed to living. She knew she had definitely made some mistakes, but she also knew that she couldn't unwind the clock that had ticked a way she wished it hadn't. She remembered how she saw the hypocrisy of her parents and committed within her heart to never live a lie herself. Owning up to her mistakes was the route she had to take and now she would make the best of a bad situation. It wouldn't be easy, but the life of one, the unborn, depended upon her. Julia was starting to realize the importance of everything she did and the impact that even just a few words, or one deed, can have upon one life, two lives, or even generations to come.

CHAPTER FOUR

Down, But Not Out

Julia went out one day to buy the groceries that they needed, and as she was walking along the sidewalk, she noticed a happy mother and father over in the city park on the other side of the street. She watched intently as their little boy, probably about four or five years old, ran around in the grass while his dad chased him. The mother looked at them playing and just laughed and laughed as the dad pretended his son was able to outrun him in their pretend races. To the little boy, it was just as real a race as any he had ever run. "What a different kind of dad that is," she thought. She wished that her own father had spent time with her like that.

Julia also thought about the way the family was there all together and how happy they appeared. Her parents always acted like they were happy when out in public, but not when no one was watching. These people seemed to have genuineness about them. She could see the look of pride the father had in his son and the look of love and trust the son had in his dad. She wished that this would be the way it would be when her baby would come soon, but she knew that it wouldn't be that way with them.

Julia's mind just wouldn't let her not picture that scene that she had just witnessed as she walked along to the store. She saw a bench coming up and decided to sit for a while. It wasn't long before the family that she had been watching came walking by going back to their vehicle. Julia overheard the husband tell his wife that he loved her. Julia tried to think about the last time Frank had told her that. "Oh yeah, once — the night I got pregnant," she thought aloud. As a tear streamed down her cheek, she felt bitterness and sadness all at once. There was more sadness than bitterness, though. What would be ahead for this tiny life that was just starting? Would this baby ever get to hear a father say, "I love you"? Would a daddy be there to even hold this baby? These were all questions that were running through her mind like wild stallions that refused to settle down. Julia just broke down there while sitting on that bench. She cried for the mistakes she had made, but she cried many times more for those she knew were inevitably ahead.

An older lady was coming down the sidewalk around the time that Julia was crying. The little lady wore a light blue shawl that she had crocheted herself and it was draped over her kyphotic back, bent over from osteoporosis. Her legs didn't carry her very fast and she aided her walking with a 4-legged cane. She had on a light pink dress and her hair was white, a beacon of light on her head guiding those who would take time to notice the wisdom that she had. The little lady, Emily, had a smile as she noticed Julia up ahead. It was as if she knew that ahead of her was another opportunity. Emily noticed that Julia was pregnant and knew that she just must stop and talk with this young person who was obviously in trouble.

"Precious, what's wrong?" asked Emily, as sweetly and lovingly as the grandmotherly type she was, could ask any question. "I sure would like to help you if I can," she offered.

"I'm okay," Julia stammered out between her tears, knowing she didn't mean what she was saying. "I've just had a bad day."

Emily didn't want to pressure her and could easily tell that she certainly was having more than just one bad day. "Honey, I'm just an old woman and all I have left is time. If you need someone to talk to, I would love to listen if you want to talk."

Julia started to tell Emily again that she would be okay and that she just wanted to be left alone, but she looked at Emily's face and saw compassion within her. Was this another refuge along Julia's path? Emily held her face down and looked up into Julia's eyes with an expression not of sadness, but one of unfortunate understanding. "What's your name?" Julia asked her to just get something out to start the conversation.

Emily told her more than just her name, hoping that her openness would stimulate Julia to be more open herself. "My name is Emily and I live just over there in those apartments. That's been my home for the last 7 years since my health got bad and my husband died. I take this walk everyday to keep my strength up. I don't get to stop and talk very often, so this is a real treat to get to talk with you."

"Well, my name is Julia. I live over there, too, in the apartments where you live. We just moved in a few weeks ago after we got married."

Emily quickly surmised the situation. Julia certainly looked more than a few weeks pregnant. "Child, where's your husband?"

"His name is Frank. I don't know where he's at today. He didn't come home last night and who knows where he is." Julia could tell that Emily knew that this wasn't a planned situation. It was an agonizing place to be. Julia wanted to turn and run from it all, but knew that she couldn't. She wouldn't be able to live with herself if she turned and tried to leave these problems, but she didn't know if she could live if she stayed. She held her face down with a profound sense of rejection by the world that she had never known before. The very things that the world told her would make her feel accepted, left her empty and hurting.

Emily held out her frail arm and Julia slumped over onto her shoulder. As Emily held her, Julia told what had happened and how things were going. Even Emily had tears in her eyes, too, because these stories seemed all too familiar to her. She had been there before, too. "Julia, you'll be okay. It'll be hard, but you'll be okay," she told her, trying to say something consoling, but knowing that life would never be what it could have been for this young one. They sat there together not saying much. There was almost an unspoken understanding between them that each knew all too well what the other had been through, or would go through. Each one of them thought back with regret at that turning point in their lives when a decision was made without much thought. It was a time for both of them when they had chosen a detour off the road that seemed, at the time, to be just another straight road, but quickly became so tortuous and confusing. There was no shoulder on the road on which to pull over and get out the map; the map was thrown away back when that narrow, straight road was left. There was nowhere to turn around and go back on this one-way highway, which led to where they did not know.

Their somber expressions soon changed as Emily tried to lighten the mood. Emily put forth a big smile, held her head up, and confidently proclaimed, "Hey, let's go and get those groceries you need—and I'm buying! We're going to get some ice cream, too, and come back and have ourselves a good time."

They got up and hurried off, both trying to forget this reminder of the past, leaving it there on that bench, at least for a while. After they did their shopping and returned, Julia just couldn't thank Emily enough for buying her groceries. Emily told her it was the least she could do to help her. They visited for another two or three hours, laughing and talking while eating a quart of ice cream together, before Emily left to go back to her apartment.

After another hour, in walked Frank with bloodshot eyes, messed up hair, and his pants had a tear on the side of one of the legs. He smelled of alcohol and his clothes were dirty, too; it was obvious to Julia he had again been out with his friends and into who knows what kind of mischief. He had some of the usual excuses about where he had been and why he didn't come home the night before, but Julia had already learned that she couldn't trust what her new husband had to say. Frank didn't talk long before going to bed where he stayed until late the next morning. When he got up the next morning, he apologized to Julia like he usually did and she reluctantly accepted it like she usually did. Both of them knew that the same scenario would be repeated again before long. Frank was briefly at home before he left to go to work at the grocery store. Julia didn't want to complain much because she was afraid she'd lose him for good if she did; she would surely have no way to support herself then. Everyone else had abandoned her, except for Elizabeth and Emily, her new friend.

The next day Julia went to see her doctor for her pregnancy checkup. "Julia, you're coming along pretty good, it appears," Dr. Tyndale informed her after the examination. "You're now at 36 weeks and it won't be long before you'll be due. Do you have everything ready that you'll need for the new baby?" Dr. Tyndale could tell that she probably didn't, but was giving Julia a chance to tell him what was happening.

"Oh, yes, I can't wait for it to be born," Julia told him with discernable nervousness in her voice. She fully well knew that she would love to wait on this if she could.

Dr. Tyndale tried to be a little more direct although he didn't want to pry too much. "Julia, is your husband ready for this baby? What's his name – Frank? I've noticed that he has never come with you to any of your appointments here."

Julia tried to make excuses for Frank like she normally did. She was really starting to resent these situations that he had caused her to be put in which she had to lie for him. "Well, Frank just has to work at the store a lot and hasn't been able to get off to come yet. He's really excited about the baby though." Julia could kick herself for saying what she just did, but she was afraid of what the doctor might think. She couldn't tell that Dr. Tyndale already knew; he had seen this same situation many times before and could easily recognize it.

Dr. Tyndale had given her a chance to talk, and he didn't want to invade her privacy too much, so he decided to maybe wait until the next visit to talk with her some more. He hoped that maybe with time and the development of more trust, she would be more honest with him. "Well, Julia, I'm glad you're both ready for this baby because you're both going to be needed a lot by this little, new life. If I can help you in any way, please let me know. The first baby is a little rough so let me know if anything comes up at all that you're unsure about. I'll see you back here again in 4 weeks."

Julia left wishing she had been honest with Dr. Tyndale. She certainly could tell that he wanted to be helpful and seemed to care. She decided that if he asked her again on the next visit, she was going to tell him about how things really were. As she was walking back to her vehicle, she noticed a piece of paper lying over on the pavement close to her car. She normally would not have paid much attention to a piece of paper that appeared to be trash, but felt inclined for some reason to go over and pick it up. It was a blue-colored, little tract. Julia took it back to her car and sat down to read what it said. On the front piece it asked, *"Are you weary and worn?"* She certainly could relate to that and opened the tract up to see what else was there. *"God is our refuge and strength, a very present help in trouble. Therefore we will not fear, even though the earth be removed, and though the mountains be carried into the midst of the sea; though its waters roar and be troubled, though the mountains shake with its swelling. There is a river whose streams shall make glad the city of God, the holy place of the tabernacle of the Most High. God is in the midst of her, she shall not be moved; God shall help her, just at the break of dawn. The nations raged, the kingdoms were moved; He uttered His voice, the earth melted. The Lord of hosts is with us; the God of Jacob is our refuge. Come, behold the works of the Lord, Who has made desolations in the earth. He makes wars cease to the end of the earth; He breaks the bow and cuts the spear in two; He burns the chariot in the fire. Be still, and know that I am God; I will be exalted among the nations, I will be exalted in the earth! The Lord of hosts is with us; the God of Jacob is our refuge"* Psalm 46 (NKJV).

Julia remembered hearing these words before when she was in church one time with her parents. Seeing this scripture made her think of her parents who used to take her to church, but now wouldn't even have anything to do with her. It also made her think more of her grandmother who had told her that she would be praying for her and who had never forsaken her because of her mistakes. Julia took the tract and slowly folded it up with care. She was slow to put it in her purse, as she was deep in thought about these words that she obviously needed to read.

CHAPTER FIVE

A New Beginning, Twice

When she got in the old Chevrolet with rust in various spots along the sides and hood, she sat still there for a while in quiet reflection. *Does God really care about me after I've done what I have? He's probably just as mad at me as my parents are. That's probably why I'm in the mess that I'm in. He's punishing me for what I've done.*

Looking through the cracks in the window, she watched some birds come and perch on some branches of a large tree nearby. They were little birds that had just started flying and they were quite clumsy. One of the little birds tried to perch on another limb, didn't quite make it, and fell to the ground. It wasn't long before a larger bird swooped down to let the little one know that it was there watching. A dog came running close and the parent bird swooped and seemed to almost holler at the dog sending it in a different direction before it saw the vulnerable, little bird on the ground. In a few minutes, the one that fell had gathered its senses and took off again up into the tree branches above; it was safe again. *You know, maybe He's trying to tell me something. Maybe He's just like that big bird that has seen His little one fall. Maybe He's waiting for me to get back up and fly back into His refuge. You know what! Maybe He's not like my parents. They deserted me after my mistake, but that bird never gave up on its own. God? Do you really care about me like that?* She knew the answer.

On the way back to her apartment, she passed someone walking on the side of the road with a duffle bag on his back and who looked pretty worn out. *That could be me there walking; I'm glad I at least have this.* She pulled over to the side of the road and told the old fellow that she could take him somewhere if he needed. He thanked her for her offer and told her that he just needed to go a little way further. As they traveled down the road, they talked about different things until he told her to turn on the next road ahead. After they got off the ramp, there was a gas station to the right where he said he wanted to get out. As he got out, he thanked her and then told her that she should go a little further down the road they had just turned off on. He said, "You'll find what you're looking for, child." Julia didn't know what to say, and when she lifted her head up to tell him bye, he was gone. Julia looked around everywhere from her car, but couldn't see him anywhere.

Julia thought that was a strange suggestion that she was given, but she decided that she would go on further down that road. It wasn't long before she came upon a little, white church building with a steeple that seemed to shoot upwards even higher than it was. In the front of the church, a white-headed, old man in overalls was trimming some bushes and doing some raking. There were two arched doors in the front and one of them was a little open as if someone had just gone inside, or someone was waiting for someone else to come. The sun was shining right behind the building and gave the place a warm, inviting look. Julia's vehicle slowed, as she felt drawn to stop. A few parking places were open out front, so Julia decided she would pull over. She thought at first she would just stop and look at the beautiful grounds of the churchyard, which looked similar to the church she used to attend. As she sat there for a minute, she decided she would get out and go look inside the church, since the door was invitingly open. When she stepped out of the car, the man that was trimming the bushes stopped his task and looked up with a welcoming smile as she slowly walked forward to the church doors. Joe had a limp that became evident to Julia as she watched him come her way to welcome her. "Hey, young lady. What's your name?"

"I'm Julia. I just wanted to look at the church. It's sort of like the one I used to go to when I was younger. What's your name?" Julia really just wanted to go inside the church, but felt obliged to at least talk for a few minutes.

Joe's smile beamed like the sun shining above and his soft, blue eyes had a caring look to them that Julia hadn't seen ever before, although his face looked similar to that fellow that she had just picked up and dropped off a little while back. "Oh, I'm just old Joe. I keep up the grounds here and just look after things. That's my little shed back there. Anytime you want to come to the church, just look for me. I'm usually doing something around here since I live back there." His face was wrinkled in a way that looked like he had had years of worry and stress, but was softened now, giving him a grandfatherly appearance. His eyes even seemed to twinkle as Julia listened and he actually seemed to Julia as though he really was concerned about her. He seemed to really want to hear what she had to say and not just listen because he felt compelled.

Joe had started living at the church many years back after an accident that left him with the limp that he had now, and left his wife and children dead. They had been traveling, and everyone was asleep except for Joe who was driving until he went to sleep, too. The truck they were driving went over an embankment and Joe was the only one who had on a seatbelt. His family was killed upon impact and he was left in critical condition in a local hospital. It took him several weeks to recover physically and even longer spiritually. He was left with feelings of guilt over what had happened that eventually helped drive him to a state of depression from which he thought he would never recover. He had lost his job because he had just quit caring anymore and was even turning to that great anesthetic of the conscience, alcohol, for at least temporary relief from the thoughts of his lost wife and children. One day when Joe was walking along the sidewalk, he met a man that could tell Joe needed a friend, and a pastor. That man was the one who later introduced him to the great Healer of wounded souls after Joe took a job there as the caretaker.

Joe asked her, "Do you want me to take you inside and show you around?"

"That would be nice if you could," Julia excitedly accepted.

Joe put down his trimming scissors and widely opened up the door so Julia could go in first. "This is an old church. It's been here a lot of years and a lot of people have come and gone through these same doors. I've cleaned and revarnished these doors several times over the years. The sanctuary is down this way. It's really beautiful."

As they walked down through the sanctuary, Julia noticed the beautiful stained glass windows and the old wooden pews that were so smooth from years of use. Down front were the altars, which had signs of wear in certain spots on the sides and top of each one. Each altar had a box of tissues by it that Julia noticed were half empty. "This really is a beautiful place. It feels so warm," Julia barely whispered as she sat down on the front pew in the middle row.

Joe noticed she kept looking down at the altar in front of her and decided he would leave so she would feel free to pray, or just think, if she wanted. "Julia, I've got a lot of work to do, so just holler for me if you need anything. I'll be right outside working on those bushes some more." Joe got up and prayed under his breath for Julia as he walked on outside.

Julia sat there for a few minutes as she thought about what the old fellow she picked up had told her about finding what she needed. She thought about the tract that she had found on the ground at the clinic just before that. She thought about how she needed that "refuge," mentioned in the scripture from Psalms. Then she remembered the words of her grandmother, Elizabeth, when she said that she would be praying for her. Julia got up and knelt at the altar in front of her. She didn't know what to say as she knelt there, but she remembered from when she was taught in Sunday school that she needed to ask for forgiveness. She thought about the mistakes that she had made and thought about the baby that would soon be with her; she laid her arms over the altar as if she was coming to the end of herself. She was coming to the end of a road that felt to her as though it was just too long and she didn't even know where the end was. It was a road that had been straight until just about a year before, but now was as crooked as could be. The detours and turns everywhere along the current path were all just too confusing. There were no rest areas and the road was cracked and worn from the other many souls that had gone down the same way. There were no lanes coming back. The only way to get off this road was to get the Great Navigator to help her find that straight road that just didn't seem to be anywhere in sight. Julia cried until she thought she could cry no more; she begged Jesus to forgive her. After she asked Him with full sincerity of heart, she felt a load lift from her shoulders that had been too much for her to carry. A peace came over her that she had never felt before as she asked Him to come into her life.

Joe had quietly come back into the church and stood silently at the back as he watched the heavenly scene in front of him. It reminded him of the time that he had surrendered himself when he was at the end of his rope. He remembered that scary moment when he knew he had to let go of the rope and fall. He just didn't know that as soon as he let go, there were hands just below him ready to take him and restore him. As Julia arose from the altar, Joe came down the middle aisle to meet her. He gave her a big hug and told her how proud he was of her making such a decision. "You didn't even need the preacher," he said jokingly. They talked for a little while, and Joe gave her some information from the church for new converts, along with telephone numbers of different people in case she needed them.

When Julia came out of the church, everything looked even brighter to her than when she went inside. She knew why she had stopped there now, and she could see God's hand leading her to that tract she had found on the ground at the clinic and then to pick up the guy on the road. Julia felt a sense of how He really did love her and she just had to go and tell the one that she knew had been praying for her so much—her grandmother, Elizabeth. Julia called her as soon as she got back home and told her what had happened to her. They talked for about an hour and then decided they would just have to meet. Julia excitedly grabbed her jacket and headed out the door, eager to tell her grandmother about what had happened to her.

She got downstairs and was heading toward her car when she felt a pain in her lower abdomen that she had never felt before. Julia knew what this must mean because it was getting time for the baby to be born. The car seemed like a long way off until she finally got close enough to reach for the handle while she walked bent over holding her belly. Julia wanted to be glad, but felt more afraid than anything right then. She tried to calm herself down enough to think about how to get to the hospital. Frank would certainly have been some help, but he wasn't at home when she had gotten there earlier and she had no idea where he was. "I sure wish he was here when I need him like this," she muttered under her breath as she was just about to the car door. Just as she was about to grab the door handle, someone reached out ahead of her and opened the door. It was none other than Emily.

"Child, what in the world are you doing out here like this by yourself? Come on 'round here 'cause I'm driving," Emily said as she helped Julia get around to the passenger side of the car. Julia didn't hesitate to take her up on her offer for help. As they drove to the hospital, Julia thanked the Lord for sending her the help she needed right at the time she needed it. *He's looking out for me just like that momma bird was looking out for her own,* she thought.

Upon arriving at the hospital, she was greeted by one of the nurses who took her to the OB/GYN suite for evaluation. Dr. Tyndale arrived to see her within the hour and, after checking her monitoring strips and examining her, told her, "Well, Julia, it looks like there'll be two of you leaving here. You're dilated to 5 centimeters already and you'll be delivering in the next several hours."

By this time, Elizabeth and William, Julia's grandparents, had heard the news from Emily and had arrived to be with them. Julia was so appreciative for their help and attention to her especially when the hours of labor just didn't seem to end. As Elizabeth wiped Julia's forehead with a wet towel to comfort her, she told her about many years ago when she was doing the same thing to Julia's mother at the time of Julia's birth. They both lamented the fact that her mom wasn't there with them and they didn't talk about Frank much. It was just understood between them that a discussion about problems right now would certainly not help during this time with its own difficulties. All that Julia could think about was how happy she was at that moment. Even though it was a moment of pain, she knew it was the beginning of a new life, and not just one. Julia had just been reborn herself and now she was giving birth. She thought about all the things she wanted to do for the baby and how she wanted to be the best mother she could be. She thought about the rejection that she felt from her own mother and how she wanted to be the most loving mother a child ever had.

Dr. Tyndale came back in to check her in an hour and announced that she was dilated then to about 6 centimeters. "Your monitoring is looking okay," he reassured Julia. He had told her earlier that she could have an epidural if she wanted it to help with the pain, but Julia had told him that she wanted to have the baby without it and didn't want to take any chances.

Elizabeth stayed with her during all the hours of labor and finally the big moment arrived. The pain was so intense Julia wondered if she had made the right decision in not getting the epidural, but it was too late now. She squeezed Elizabeth's hand just about into two. Dr. Tyndale offered to do a pudendal block for at least some relief and Julia screamed out her consent. The baby was already on the way out and everything was progressing well. In only a few more minutes, Sarah Dupree was born into this world. It was a world that would bring her a lot of heartache, although she didn't know what was ahead of her. Dr. Tyndale brought Sarah for Julia to hold. Julia instantly formed a bond with this new life that nothing could ever break. She looked into those new, little eyes and saw nothing but hope and the promise of something better. She touched Sarah's tiny fingers and hands and just couldn't believe how small they were next to hers. All the problems she was having with Frank were forgotten when looking at what they had together now. Having this new life was like getting to start over again. She hoped that maybe seeing Sarah would bring Frank to his senses.

Julia had a small tear from the delivery and, after Dr. Tyndale had repaired her, they wheeled her and the baby out of the suite into the hall toward the rooms. William anxiously was awaiting them and was glad to see his new great-granddaughter was okay. As Julia was coming into the room, she was surprised to see someone else standing in the room: it was Frank. Julia didn't know what to say at first when she saw him. She was upset that he wasn't there earlier when she needed him. He hadn't been there a lot for her, but he was there then. Julia's initial frozen expression, while she was deciding how she would react, quickly changed to an expression of rejoicing when Frank smiled at her.

CHAPTER SIX

Frank Sees Beyond Himself

Frank saw the new baby's face and was in a state of awe. He could hardly believe that the little life in front of him was his daughter. Sarah's eyes looked like Julia's and her high cheekbones favored Frank's. After the minute or two it took Frank to get his mouth closed and come to his senses, he was grinning from ear to ear. He sat down by Julia and didn't know what to say at first. He finally leaned over and gave her a hug and then looked into her eyes and told her, "Julia, I'm sorry for the way I've been. This baby is the best thing that's ever happened to me. Well, besides you. I just really wanted to say that I love you."

Julia was the one then who didn't know what to say. She had been wondering what was going to happen to their new marriage because Frank had been acting like he just didn't care. Hearing those three words meant more to her than anything ever could have. She pondered whether this could be what would bring Frank around to being the responsible husband, and now father, that he needed to be. Julia looked back into Frank's eyes and cried tears of joy when she told him, "I love you, too."

Standing in the room around them, Emily, Elizabeth, and William, had longed to see what they had just beheld in front of them. A relationship was mended through a forgiving spirit readily evident in Julia. Emily and Elizabeth gave each other a hug as they thought about their own marriages; the former, over, and the latter, continuing. The nurse in the room, too, could not help but be affected by such a show of love for one another. Everyone there had a smile on their face as though each had another loved one on their mind, also. "Well, what y'all say we leave these love birds alone for a while with their new, little Sarah," William offered. They left them then. On the second day, Julia, Frank, and Sarah left the hospital together knowing they were going to never be the same.

In the next few months, Sarah brought such joy into the lives of everyone she knew. Frank and Julia's relationship was stronger because Frank realized what a great responsibility that he had now. Frank's parents hadn't been there very much for him, and he determined that he would be a better parent than what he had. Julia could hardly believe the way that Frank was changing before her eyes since Sarah came along. He wasn't home much before, but now, as soon as work was over, he was home with them. A lot of times Frank would even bring home a little toy or something that he had picked up after work just for his little Sarah. Julia came into the living room often and found Frank holding her in his arms so quietly, gazing into her eyes with a look of wonder, joy, and amazement in his face.

Julia and Frank spent more time talking to each other now, and not at one another. Frank had been able to tell something different about Julia, too. He knew it wasn't just due to Sarah's arrival although it certainly accounted for some of it. While they were talking one night, Frank asked Julia about why she seemed different. Julia told him about her experience that day at the church. She told him about the hitchhiker and about old Joe, too. They both sensed a need for positive influences in Sarah's life, as well as their own. After discussing it for a while, Julia convinced Frank that they needed to start attending church and they decided to pay a visit to the little, white church that Julia had come across recently. Julia found the materials that Joe had given her when she had visited the church. She decided she'd call the church to let Joe know they were coming. When Joe heard the news, he was ecstatic. Joe told her that he had been just hoping and praying that everything would work out okay for them. Julia was excited about this new life opening up before her.

On the first service that they attended, the warmth they felt when they came into the building astonished them. Joe introduced them to everyone and Sarah's little, fat cheeks were pinched and kissed so much they stayed red for an hour. After the song service was over, the dark-haired, tall, slender pastor emerged for the Sunday morning message. Rev. Mickey Davis was soft spoken, but direct and bold at the same time. Everyone called him Bro. Mickey and he was a pastor's pastor if there ever was one. Bro. Mickey had been at the church for many years shepherding them all the best he could with the Lord's help. When he saw Frank, Julia, and Sarah sitting on the back pew that morning, he didn't tarry long before going to welcome them. Frank never had cared too much for preachers, but he really felt like Bro. Mickey cared about him.

The sermon that morning was just what they needed to hear. They listened intently as the pastor brought to life the story of the woman caught in the act of adultery. Bro. Mickey had tears in his eyes as he expressed how the woman must have felt to have her sins forgiven and avoided losing her life at the hands of the crowd that dragged her before Jesus. He cried out loud as he expressed the woman's relief she must have felt, "Why did this man care for me?

Why did he not condemn me with the rest? What have I done to deserve this love for me?" The congregation realized, like they never had before, the woman's gratitude for what Jesus had done for her.

Julia wept as she thought about the forgiveness she had experienced and she silently prayed throughout the message that Frank would see his need for Christ, too. Julia watched as Frank squirmed in his seat. He seemed to get a little angry in his facial expressions at first. Bro. Mickey could tell that Frank was uneasy and was under conviction; he walked the aisles and frequently stopped at the pew where Frank and Julia sat so he could be sure Frank was not distracted. Frank became so uncomfortable that he just appeared miserable. The best thing he heard was when the service was coming to a close and the invitational hymn was announced. Frank thought that he could certainly endure a little longer, but Bro. Mickey had been a pastor for a long time and was experienced in picking just the right song and saying the right words to bring those stubborn, die-hard, hold-out-no-matter-what-it-takes souls to their knees.

That hymn seemed so long to him as he stood there while the congregation sung "I Surrender All." The first verse was coming to a close and Frank already had a little bit of sweat on his brow. He hoped Bro. Mickey would stop the invitation with just one verse when no one came down to the altar, but that just wasn't to be. Bro. Mickey had glanced Frank's way long enough to see he was certainly under conviction. The verses to the hymn seemed to last forever to Frank; Bro. Mickey paused the song after each verse trying to convince the one he knew needed to come forward.

The good pastor prayed as he stood there for the Holy Spirit to continue to work in their midst. Frank was in turmoil as the forces of darkness gave him excuse after excuse to wait until later. The second verse came and was just getting over when a tear from Frank's right eye started rolling down his cheek. He tried the best he could to keep anyone from noticing the state he was in. The third verse finally began after Bro. Mickey tried to say the right words to convince Frank to surrender.

Julia couldn't help but notice how Frank was struggling and she gently took his hand. Frank looked up at her as his head was bowed and silently consented as Julia looked into his eyes with her head nodding toward the altar. Frank felt a sense of release even as soon as he stepped out into the aisle. The chains that were holding him in his seat were broken and he shot down that aisle as fast as he could go.

Julia and Frank prayed together with Bro. Mickey for quite a while and the church family patiently waited and sang hymns. One of the ladies that sat next to them held Sarah up so she could see them down in the front. When the altar service was over, they stood by the altar with the pastor as the whole congregation filed by to greet them and welcome them to the family.

CHAPTER SEVEN

Their New Life Together

They hadn't been happier together ever before. Frank was so happy that he couldn't help sharing with others his newfound life. The people he worked with could tell there was something different about him. Frank was eager to learn more about his faith and regularly attended church meetings with Julia. He even took part in plays the church did during the holidays and everyone commented on how much they both had added to the church and its ministry with the community. Bro. Mickey was so proud of how much they both were growing, too, and he, not infrequently, stopped by their house just to visit and encourage them.

Sarah was flourishing with the attention she was getting from both of her parents. Frank came home a lot of times from the grocery store with special treats just for her and she could see how much he loved Julia. One time he brought home some fish for supper and Julia said she wanted to have some hush puppies to serve with the meal. Frank left to go get some frozen ones at the store and when he returned Sarah kept looking around everywhere. Julia noticed that Sarah was looking for something she couldn't find and asked her what in the world she was trying to find. Sarah told her, "Daddy get hush puppy. Where puppy? He hush?" Frank and Julia laughed at her interpretation of what hush puppies were and patiently explained what they were.

Frank was doing well at work and was promoted to assistant manager when Sarah was two years old. Julia was certainly glad to get the extra income for the family as she had been staying home to raise Sarah. They were even gladder the extra income was there when Julia learned that another baby was on the way. Frank and Julia had discussed whether or not they wanted to have any more children and decided that they wanted to wait until they had their financial situation under better control. They had both learned that they wanted things to go as God would have it for them, but recognized it would be better for them to wait. This was unexpected, but they both really wanted a sibling for Sarah.

"If we keep waiting for the best time, we'll never have another one," Frank told Julia.

"Yeah, we better be glad He's blessed us this way. A lot of people never even have a chance to have any children," Julia said in a thankful way.

Frank and Julia were surely a lot different now as compared to before when she was pregnant with Sarah. They looked upon this child, as not something that was a problem for them or a burden, but an event they had now recognized was a miracle in and of itself. Every night before they went to sleep, they prayed for the baby that wasn't even born yet. They focused on praying for every aspect of the baby's new life that it would be directed by Him. Julia was much more concerned about how she ate and kept herself as healthy as she could this time. She recognized that even though she didn't care much last time, it was to God's credit that everything turned out okay for Sarah.

"Frank, why are some babies born with health problems as a result of their mothers' lifestyles, while others are born without problems to mothers in the same situation?" Julia asked him once. They both thought about the question for a moment and couldn't come up with a reasonable answer. The thought gave them a greater sense of gratitude than they had before. They still didn't have very much in the way of material possessions, but Julia was sincere when she told Frank, "We sure are blessed."

Emily had remained a close friend to Julia and Frank during the years and they regularly relied upon her to even help baby-sit sometimes. Emily had really enjoyed seeing the young family grow. She was thrilled to see them staying together through those tough first years and had spent much time interceding for them in her prayers. Emily's health had been declining during that time, too, although. She had heart failure and diabetes. Those walks outside that she loved had to stop a couple of years before, and she was pretty much confined to her apartment now. The help she had given to so many others in the apartment complex was now being returned to her. People stopped by regularly to see if she needed something since they were going to the grocery store or drug store. Some would come get her and wheel her around outside in her wheelchair so she could see the birds, the children, and get some fresh air.

Emily never missed a moment to share something that she thought would help someone. She had helped Julia so much during a time when Julia didn't know which way to turn. Frank had learned of Emily's kindnesses when he wasn't being the husband he should have been; he regularly expressed his gratitude to her for befriending Julia. Both Frank and Julia had noticed how Emily's health had declined and how slow she was getting around. Julia went to visit her one Saturday morning and could not get her to answer the door. Emily was always home so this was certainly unusual. Julia went to the manager's office and asked someone who came to let her inside. Upon entering the door, there was Emily lying on the floor of the kitchen. She made no response to them coming inside and Julia was just beside herself to see her dear friend in this bad condition. The apartment manager called the ambulance and Emily was taken to the hospital.

Emily was diagnosed with dehydration and had a severe infection in her bladder that had become systemic. They gave her intravenous fluids and antibiotics, but she had been in the apartment on the floor far too long. Julia stayed by her side from the time she was admitted and tended to her every need the best that she knew how. Emily became responsive enough to recognize Julia and thanked her for caring for her so much. She told her how much she had prayed for her, Frank, and Sarah, and how much she loved them all. Julia kept trying to encourage Emily by telling her that she was going to get better and would go back home. Emily would just smile and say that she was going to go home, but Julia didn't quite understand that Emily had a different home in mind.

Emily had told them over the years how much she missed her husband who had died. Julia and Emily had become such close friends because of their common past. Emily shared with Julia how she had become pregnant with her son while she and John were dating. They had married precipitously and their parents had almost disowned them. They had a tough time getting by those first few years and had been in a similar situation as Frank and Julia. Their son had died because of a premature birth, but they decided to go ahead and name him anyway. His name was Mark, and they buried him in the city cemetery where her husband John was laid many years later; another spot had been reserved next to John's. They never had any other children.

Julia thought about all the good times they had shared together and especially about what a servant Emily had been for so long. Late that second night in the hospital, as Julia was wiping Emily's brow with a cool, wet cloth, Emily started talking and said, "I see someone. Mark, is that you honey? I've missed you so much. Oh, and John, it's you, too, my love. Dear Jesus, my Lord, I can see you. Oh, I can't believe this! I'm finally home." The last few words were barely audible to Julia as she struggled to hear every word that was said as Emily slipped from this life to the next. Julia had never heard anything like this, and it cemented her faith like nothing ever had before. She cried for her loss of such a good friend and cried for joy that Emily was now complete and well. Brother Mickey preached the funeral that was attended by over a hundred people from the apartment complex. All of them shared with each other how much Emily had helped them over the years.

After the funeral, Julia eventually got back into her usual routines. Her clinic visits with Dr. Tyndale were going well and no complications had emerged. Julia kept the apartment spotless except for when Sarah had extra energy. Sarah was learning a lot because of all the extra time Julia spent with her at home teaching her as much of everything as she could. Sarah was getting ready to start the first grade at school soon. She was nervous, but excited, too. Julia had already taught her the alphabet and how to write her name.

Julia took every opportunity to help other people in the area just as Emily had done. When she knew of someone new moving in, she was the first to go and introduce herself, along with a fresh, baked apple pie. Julia helped baby-sit for other couples there and even learned how to knit several different items that she sold to make extra money to give to the church missionary fund. She also hosted a ladies' prayer meeting in her home on Tuesday nights that had grown to include twelve women in the first year of its inception. The ladies rejoiced regularly in prayers that had been answered.

CHAPTER EIGHT

Tragedy Strikes

Frank was still working at the grocery store and was now the manager of it. He had added responsibilities with the promotion and took his job very seriously. Many people in the area had come to trust and respect Frank. His hard work was evident in every department of the store. The other employees looked up to him as someone to emulate. The store was in excellent financial shape. Frank's assistant manager, Tom, had to miss work one Saturday night and Frank came in to work for him. After the store closed for the night, Frank stayed late finishing up everything for the deposit. Everything checked out fine. He locked up and headed out for the bank.

Usually he had someone go with him to the bank, but he didn't that night. When he got there, everything looked like it normally did and he got out of his car to go put the money in the night depository drop box. Not long after he got out of his car, a man in dark clothes emerged from the shadows and started approaching Frank. Frank heard him coming, but was too far from his car to run back. The man told Frank to "hold it," but Frank ran toward the bank to try to get the money into the depository. Frank had just pulled open the door when he felt a surge of heat go through his chest like he had never felt before. A split second later, he heard the sound of the shot, and then fell to the ground in a rapidly enlarging pool of blood. Frank leaned over and saw the crimson flow of life running away from his body.

The robber ran up to Frank's dying body and grabbed the moneybag lying right under the depository box. Just as he was reaching for the bag, he told Frank, "You fool! All you had to do was give me the bag and I wouldn't have had to shoot you!" That great robber of men's souls had tried his hardest to take Frank's soul, and had failed in the end. Even though Frank's physical life was being taken by this human robber, who was after something that neither of them could take with them, Frank decided that he could offer this robber something else that no other human could take away.

Frank mustered enough strength to reply to the robber solemnly, "Jesus loves you anyway." The robber couldn't stand to hear that and ran away as fast as he could. Frank only lived another minute. During that minute, he could only think of Julia, Sarah, and the new baby that was on the way. He wanted so much to tell them bye, but was instead there to face death alone, as it possibly would appear to some observers. Frank wasn't alone although. He had begun to see angels at his side, felt a sense of love and peace like none he had experienced before, and then saw the brightest light before he passed from this side to the other.

Julia just couldn't bear it all when she found out the awful news late that night. She had been frantically calling around trying to find Frank when he was so late in coming home. The police had called her and asked her to meet them. She knew that something had to be terribly wrong. They brought her into the morgue to identify this bluish, pale body. It was the worst horror that she had ever had to face when they pulled back that sheet and she saw her Frank there. She fell over onto him and hugged him so tightly, as she wailed to God, "Why? Why, God? Why?"

Everything lately had been so perfect and seemed to be finally going so well. She wondered why it couldn't stay that way. Had they done something wrong? Was God punishing her for the past? Why couldn't Frank have just given the robber the moneybag? Why didn't God protect him from harm? Why did Tom have to miss work that night and Frank have to work instead? Why did Emily have to die, too, and now leave her in this hard and cold world all alone? She remembered scripture that says: "*And we know that all things work together for good to those who love God, to those who are called according to His purpose*" (Romans 8:28/NKJV). How could this be something good for her when she was going to be alone with Sarah and another child was coming soon? What good was going to come out of this? All of these questions and many more ran through her mind in a short period of time that seemed like an eternity as Julia continued to hold Frank's bloody, stiffened body.

The police officer there couldn't help but to become teary eyed as he saw what love she had for this person whom he had never known. After they had been there several minutes, he slowly walked over, placed his arm on her shoulder, and quietly asked Julia if she was ready to come down the hall to let them know where to send the body. She didn't want to think about that either. Julia wanted to take Frank home with her. The thought even came that maybe if she held him longer he would come back. She knew that she would have to leave him there on that cold, metal table. This couldn't be real, she thought. She slowly let Frank slip out of her shaking hands, and then turned and ran out of the room.

She couldn't see Him, but the same One who wept in the Bible when confronted with the grief of His creation, also wept there as He saw Julia, a child of His, hurting. Only when Julia could be face to face with Him one day would she completely understand the answers to all of the questions that she had then.

It was all just too much for her. Only a few hours before, her life was totally different. In one short moment, her life was changed forever. No, the world had changed forever. Julia knew that every person has an effect on another person who in turn affects someone else. Each person leaves some type of impression and effect on those whom they meet and the chain of interactions affects us all in some way. She felt a sense of loss that she couldn't even start to measure. She felt just like the center of her being had been pulled out and put up somewhere that she didn't know where to find. She would find the answers slowly with the help of friends, family, and God. What lay ahead she didn't know, and that was the biggest question of all.

Sarah had gone with her to the station, but had stayed in the office with another policeman while her mom went to that dreadful room. Julia had no idea what to say to Sarah at the station and wanted to keep her composure in front of her until they could get back home. Even though Sarah was a child, she knew that something was not right at all. Sarah noticed her mother's facial expressions, her unusual quietness, and could easily see the signs of all of the weeping that had occurred. When Julia got home, she had no idea how she would explain this to Sarah. She suddenly had so many things to do that she didn't know what to do first.

She needed help to be able to get through this, and the first person she called was Bro. Mickey. This was her trusted pastor, and his wife, Grace, came with him to Julia's apartment to help get her through this tough time. All three of them sat down in the living room with Sarah to try to explain to her what had happened. Bro. Mickey told Sarah that her daddy had gone to a better place and that it was such a good place, a place that was beyond anything that they could imagine, and that he couldn't come back. He told her that God wanted her daddy there; He had a special assignment for him, and needed him early. All of that seemed to ease the tension of the truth. When she got older and was ready, Julia could tell her the grim details of what had happened.

Sarah still did not comprehend what had taken place and later asked when her daddy was going to be home. Earlier that day, Sarah had brought some shoes into the kitchen where a lot of people were gathered and asked one of the ladies if they were her daddy's shoes. Julia hated to tell her that it was the shoes of one of the other men who had come over to visit during their time of bereavement. Sarah had slowly walked away in embarrassment of her mistake. She just wanted to find something of his, something that maybe would bring him back. *He just couldn't be really gone. This couldn't be real. Here's his shoes, see.*

That night, Julia had gone to bed emotionally exhausted and was awakened when Sarah climbed up into the bed with her as she cried, asking again where her daddy had gone. Julia just tried to keep reminding them both that they would see him again one day, but that he wasn't able to come back. They held on to each other that night and cried each other to sleep. The darkness of the night hardly compared to the darkness that had come across their spirits. Both of them hoped that they would awaken in the morning and find out that it was all just a bad dream.

The next morning, William and Elizabeth, her grandparents, came along with her reluctant parents, Susan and Cecil, to try to help. The funeral was going to be the next day and it was an uphill struggle for Julia to do every task that was required of her. She had to decide how she was going to live now that Frank wasn't there to make the money to pay the bills. They wouldn't be able to stay where they were unless Julia worked, and then how would she take care of Sarah and the new baby that was coming?

Cecil hadn't changed much since Julia used to live at home. He just had to remind her that none of this would have happened if she had just listened to him in the beginning. This certainly wasn't going to help matters now and it surely wasn't as if Julia didn't know the mistakes that she had made. From Cecil's attitude, one would think he had never made any mistakes. Susan didn't offer much tangible support either. Elizabeth, however, was as gracious as usual and provided the unconditional love that Julia needed right then. After William and Elizabeth had talked about it, they offered to let Julia move in with them so she would have the help she needed. Julia readily accepted their compassionate offer.

The funeral was so tough for them all, but it wasn't any tougher for anyone more than Julia. She came into the funeral home that morning knowing that she would have to greet all of those people. All of them would understandably want to express their sorrow, but Julia wondered how she'd make it through each time someone would again, and then again, and again bring up Frank's life and death, discussing how they would miss him. But Julia made up her mind and got herself strapped in for the emotional roller coaster ride.

Julia was in a state of shock initially, but had to handle the arrangements anyway. She had picked out the casket the day before the funeral, and now she saw him lying in it as though he were asleep. Julia snapped a few Polaroids so that the kids could one day see their dad in his casket when they would understand better. She stood there so strong on the outside in front of everyone, but on the inside she was just about to collapse. She didn't really have a lot of time to think about what Frank's death meant. She didn't really have a lot of time to realize that this wasn't a movie; it wasn't a nightmare of a dream; it was real. It had happened and Frank was really in that casket in front of her. When the reality of it all hit home, Julia had to summon all the strength that she could muster and all that God would give her.

Little Sarah greeted everyone at the funeral with an uncertainty about her. She knew something wasn't right and knew her dad was up in that "bed-with-a-lid" on the table; she watched as everyone kept coming up to look at him and some would turn away in tears. Her little, blue eyes didn't have the usual amount of sparkle that they normally had before. She had on a new, dark blue dress with a bow on the back. Her blonde hair was so pretty and fixed so neatly that it was surely unusual for her. She was accustomed to wearing her regular clothes and running around the house with her hair all messed up from constant playing. Sarah noticed that everyone at the funeral seemed so somber and different than anything that she had experienced before. She wondered if she would always feel that way and if everyone would always seem as sad as they seemed then. Her world wasn't as secure as she was accustomed to it being, and this scared her more than anything.

At the burial, Sarah sat over in those special chairs under the tent that never feel special to the ones sitting in them. She sat next to her mother and brother with her grandparents and great grandparents behind them. The words from the pastor attempted to comfort all, but were only minimally heard by Sarah. She was in her own world of thought about what this all meant. After the prayer, she got up and walked several yards away from the tent to be alone. She looked back at the somber expressions on all of the faces and never could remember a more sad time in her life so far.

One of the ladies that attended the funeral brought over a little, artificial, dove that she had gotten from off one of the many flower arrangements at the burial site. Sarah just looked at it and wondered if she should take it or not. It was to her as if she was taking something that belonged to her dad; she wondered if it might be better to let it stay there and be a comfort to him. The lady told her to take it home with her and keep it so that she could remember her dad every time she saw it. Sarah reluctantly took the dove and treasured it for many years to come. The little, white dove became yellowed in color over the years and some who saw it thought it needed to be thrown away. They didn't know the significance that the little dove had to her. Throwing it away to her would be like throwing away her memory.

CHAPTER NINE

Nowhere to Go, But Up

Julia and Sarah were settling in with Elizabeth and William at their home. Julia coped with the situation best by staying busy. She was always doing something. She just couldn't feel comfortable with relaxing because this gave her too much time to think. She didn't want to think too hard about the future because it was so uncertain at that time. The folks at church told her to trust in the Lord, and she was learning the hard way how to do that. It was something much easier to say than to do.

She questioned God just as any human being would do. She couldn't understand the answer to the question of why and He told her that she wasn't made to understand everything now, but that one day she would understand it all. She had to trust, be patient, and wait on Him. She couldn't understand the answer to the question of how Sarah was going to be taken care of best this way, and He told her that He would guide the way and He would take care of them both. She had to trust, be patient, and wait on Him. She couldn't understand how she would endure this trial, and He told her that "we also glory in tribulations, knowing that tribulation produces perseverance; and perseverance, character; and character, hope" (Romans 5: 3-4, NKJV). She had to trust, be patient, and wait on Him. She questioned Him on how this could possibly be good, and He told her that "all things work together for good to those who love God, to those who are the called according to His purpose" (Romans 8:28/ NKJV). She had to trust, be patient, and wait on Him.

Julia learned a lot through persevering, and sometimes even blindly trusting Him when she couldn't see any light at the end of the almost pitch black tunnel. She could only see what was right in front of her. He did take care of her and Sarah, just as He had promised. They didn't have all of their wants, but they had all of their needs. Julia wasn't the same person that she had been before Frank's death. Nothing would ever be the same, but she remembered that no one promised her that things would always stay the same. She realized that she had no right to expect life to be like she wanted it to be. She was the clay and He was the potter; she knew that she shouldn't be upset with the vessel He saw fit to create and use in a certain way. She realized that she had no right to decide what was fair and right; these decisions must be left up to Him, the only just judge. She had no where to go and no where to look for the help she needed; she had to look up, and He looked down in compassion, hearing her prayers.

Julia joined a support group composed of various persons in the community who had also lost their spouses. They helped each other do a lot of the things for the kids that were harder to do when with just one parent. It also provided a forum for them to discuss problems and hear from others with more experience on how to handle them. They got together often just to spend time with each other and give the children activities together.

One of the people that Julia met in the support group was Sharon. She was "57 years young", as she liked to put it, and never had anything but a smile on her face. Sharon was one of those people in a group who tend to just light it up with such a vibrant personality. Sharon could tell right off the bat that Julia was down and she made it her mission to remedy that as soon as possible. Sharon first saw Julia from across the room at one of their gatherings.

"Hey there, young lady! I'm Sharon. What's your name?" she bubbled out with a big smile while graciously extending her hand.

"I'm Julia. It's nice to meet you," Julia said with a weak voice and uninterested tone. Julia had already put up an invisible wall with others and was very timid about letting anyone inside. She didn't offer any details about herself for fear of being hurt. If anyone was going to be her friend, it would be someone who purposefully set out to do so. The old saying about never judging a person's walk until you've walked a mile in their shoes was something that Sharon understood. She could recognize what Julia needed because she had been in the same kind of trouble and had been alone before also. The only person, who Julia would allow to know much about her, or help her, would be someone who had shown to her that they could be trusted. Someone that she could trust to be open and vulnerable with was someone with whom she could have a real relationship.

They discussed those usual small talk items that everyone usually shares back and forth initially, before getting to the heart of the matter. Since this was a support group for widows and children, it would be natural to share why each other was there in the group. Julia hated to talk about the topic and didn't offer much information.

Sharon could tell that she needed to really break the ice with Julia, so she told her about her wonderful husband, Richard, who was taken from her after 24 years of marriage. That was ten years ago now. He was diagnosed with leukemia and only lived about a year after diagnosis. It was a shock to them both, but they did have some time to spend with each other knowing the inevitable was going to come. They had enough time to tell each other how much they loved one another and to talk about all those wonderful times that they had shared together. Sharon had a lot of great times with Richard and they had raised three children together.

After they talked for awhile, Julia felt more at ease and could tell that Sharon really understood what she had been going through all this time. Julia then told Sharon about it all and how tough it had been. What a comfort it was for someone else to be there to help her with this. Julia couldn't expect Sarah to understand completely how she felt, although they did share with each other. They each had different needs that were unmet since Frank was gone.

One activity that Sharon and Julia liked to do together was aerobics at a local church fellowship hall. It was great exercise, but it was also a good way to work off some stress. They met each Thursday evening at 6:30 and sweated out a lot of their frustrations and anxieties for the week. Sarah was old enough to participate some, and everyone enjoyed seeing someone so young in there who didn't creak and crack with each joint movement.

Julia had social security benefits after Frank's death and did not have to work outside the home which was especially helpful with the little one on the way. It also helped that Frank did love her enough to have provided life insurance just in case something happened to him. Julia had received a check for $100,000 which she put into the bank and decided to keep it there until the children were older. This would provide a financial foundation for their education and the beginning of their lives when they were grown.

She continued aerobics until the pregnancy made it uncomfortable. Other activities in which Julia participated included helping keep up the house, since they were living with William and Elizabeth, and learning how to sew. She didn't have a lot of experience before with seamstress work, but Sharon did. They worked together making new clothes for the upcoming addition to the family, and also for Sarah and themselves.

Julia also had to keep up with the visits to see Dr. Tyndale. He was very supportive of her and always inquired as to how she was handling everything. Julia was nervous about this new baby coming since Frank wouldn't be there. She knew that it is always best for a child to have a mother and a father. Dr. Tyndale could discern her anxieties and told her everything positive that he could think. When the most recent ultrasound was done, he told her everything was okay and he wanted to know if Julia would like to know the sex of the child. Julia hesitated in replying, but then told him she did want to know. Julia hoped that it would be a boy because she wanted to name him Frank, Jr. When Dr. Tyndale told her that it would indeed be a boy, she was elated. She thought of all those great times that Sarah would have with her new little brother. The only negative thing that Julia could think of was that he wouldn't be able to get hand-me-down clothes from Sarah.

Knowing that she would be having Frank, Jr., made her feel better to some degree. She would have a reminder of her husband and she could tell him one day what a great father he had. When she told Sarah about her new brother, Sarah was excited, too, and ran around the house with baby dolls, already pretending that she was holding him. There was no where to go but upward, and things were starting to look upward to her. It was about time for a change and Julia thanked Him for providing her this blessing in the midst of such a hardship.

CHAPTER TEN

The Growing Years

Sarah was three years old when Frank, Jr., was born after another uneventful delivery with the able help of Dr. Tyndale. Julia was recovering and settling into a weekly routine. Frank, Jr., required a lot of time, of course, since he was a newborn. With Sarah being older, she was able to help with taking care of everything. She enjoyed getting to have extra responsibilities and privileges that Julia entrusted her with doing. It was like a reward for her to do something that her mom asked of her, and then get a big hug with the feeling of acceptance and love that came with it. Julia made sure that Sarah knew just how much that she was loved and was cognizant of the fact that the time it took to take care of Frank, Jr., could make Sarah feel less wanted.

Sarah just loved it when Julia would let her go get the baby and hold him for a while. She had played with baby dolls so much and this was just something beyond belief to her to get to hold a real baby. Sarah learned how to change the diapers and had fun helping Julia with this. She watched her mom as she sang lullabies to him at night; the next night, she wanted to sing little Frank, Jr., to sleep. Sarah became really protective of him and it was like she thought he was her child. Julia was just amazed at how much Sarah enjoyed helping take care of him. She really needed the help anyway and having her own daughter care so much about her little brother made things so much easier.

They usually just called him Frank since his dad wasn't there, unless Julia was upset when his entire full name, Frank Paul Dupree, Jr., would be called out in a very stern, I-mean-business voice. When Julia looked at Frank she could see his father in a lot of the things that he did. The way that he rubbed his nose, the way that he looked at her when he wanted something, and the way that he looked when he knew he had done something wrong and didn't want her to know. He was a quiet child who didn't cry a lot or make a lot of noise or fuss, usually. That certainly didn't bother Julia. He looked really funny a few times when Sarah was learning how to put on diapers and had both sides fastened to one leg. It didn't bother him, and he ran around all over the house like that just laughing up a storm.

When Sarah was five and Frank was two years old, they got into a routine of playing with the broom in the house as if it were a horse. Sarah and Frank would ride with it bucking, snorting, and turning over in their vivid imagination. Sarah would play a little rough with Frank sometimes, but if Frank fell or got hurt, she was the first to get him to Julia to help see what was wrong.

Julia just loved seeing them so happy as they ran together through the house on that broom. "What a simple toy," she thought, "and it didn't even cost anything extra." Julia had to watch every penny to make things last from month to month. She wished that they had been able to live by themselves out in the country where she might have been able to have done some gardening and have had something to sell for extra money. It was so gracious of Elizabeth and William to let them stay there with them. Julia would have had a hard time trying to pay for a house on her own through that kind of work.

Frank wasn't yet old enough for chores around the house, but Sarah was responsible for making her bed, helping with feeding Frank, changing his diapers, and helping wash the dishes every night. Julia regularly showed Sarah a little more about cooking and preparing meals. Helping to set the table was something Sarah liked to do, also. When they would sit down to eat, Julia had already taught them early how to bow their heads and say the blessing. Sarah would say the prayer most of the time and whenever she did, she had taught Frank how to say "Amen" at the end.

Another ritual at meal time was getting Frank to eat his vegetables, which he hated to do. Sarah and Julia would usually try making a game out of it to get him to eat those little, green, round peas that he hated the most. They would try bribing him by telling him that if he ate a certain number of peas, then he could have something he liked more – two saltine crackers with peanut butter on the tops and a glass of chocolate milk.

It seemed like there was always someone having a birthday party. Julia had made friends with another family in the area with whom she went to church; Joann and Sonny had three children, Greg, Todd, and Mallory at ages seven, five, and three. They all got together each time one of their children had a birthday. Cake, gifts, and Kool-Aid were the usual fare. Greg liked being the show-off of the group and always had some way to get the attention focused on him. Todd was Sarah's age, and they had a good time playing house with one another. Mallory and Frank were their children in their imaginary family. They tried to get Greg to be the grandfather, but he was "too grown-up for such nonsense."

Julia and Joann had gotten to be good friends and they even disciplined each other's children when they had to do so. Julia had learned more and more about sewing and made outfits for Frank and Sarah often. Especially each Easter, they had two new matching outfits made. The kids hated having to pose for pictures on Easter morning before church, and Frank usually had to be put in place several times for the picture with his pouty face after being scolded for being so restless. He was the smallest and tried to get away with as much as he could. Julia helped Joann with alterations often and taught her a lot of the sewing skills that she had learned.

When the summer of Frank's third year came, Julia and Joann decided it was time for teaching all the kids how to swim. Sonny told Joann that they could learn how to swim easily if they were taught like he was. "Just take them down to a good, wide, deep river in the area and throw 'em in. They'll learn really quick that way," he said. Joann was aghast at such an idea and Julia's mouth almost hit the floor. Sonny was wise enough to know he wouldn't be able to try that old-fashioned method of teaching swimming with these two mother hens. They eventually found a lady in the area that had a pool at home and taught lessons there.

Sarah did well with learning how to swim since she was accustomed to following instructions from her mom, but Frank didn't do as well. He liked having his own way and would cry every time the teacher wouldn't hold him in the water. The teacher thought she'd get him to cooperate better by telling him that he could ride a pony if he would learn to swim from one side of the pool to the other by the end of the lessons. Frank really wanted to ride that pony, but it wasn't enough to convince him that he needed to swim across that long stretch of water in the pool. Greg had already learned how to swim on his own with some of his friends. Mallory and Todd did pretty well learning how to swim and weren't much trouble. Later that summer, Joann and Julia found a creek close to the house where they could take the kids to swim after they all learned how, and Julia kept working with Frank until he learned.

That summer was just great, and it was good for both families. Julia was so glad to have the blessing of a good friend in Joann with whom she could share her thoughts and problems. She talked with Elizabeth some, but having someone her own age as her friend made her more comfortable. Joann and Sonny had a few squabbles from time to time, and Julia was usually able to help Joann figure out how to get things resolved. Many times Julia felt lonely and just needed someone to talk to about whatever came to mind, or a shoulder to cry on when those dark spells of missing Frank came around. They were two friends who stood with one another, and it was hard for them both to imagine a day in time when finding a friend like that would be difficult. Julia hadn't felt that close to anyone since her good friend, Emily, had died.

Elizabeth and William were really pleased, and even joyous, over how Julia and the kids were healing emotionally. It had been quite a while now since Frank had been killed—over three and a half years. They were glad to have had the time to spend with them all, but felt that it was time for Julia to consider dating someone. When Elizabeth told her that she thought she "should think about meeting someone," Julia was not very receptive to the idea at all. Julia wanted what was best for Sarah and Frank above all; she didn't think at first that what would be good for her might would be good for the kids, also, or so she thought.

CHAPTER ELEVEN

Julia and Chris

Joann and Julia usually met each Thursday afternoon for coffee or tea. Elizabeth had called Joann the day before and told her that she wanted her to bring up the idea to Julia on Thursday. Joann was really excited about the prospects of being a matchmaker and already had someone in mind that she was hoping to introduce to Julia. After their first cup of coffee that afternoon, Joann asked Julia when she thought she might be ready to consider meeting someone. "Did you and 'Liz talk about this because she brought this same topic up with me the other day? I bet she called you; didn't she?" Julia wasn't about to let them pull something on her. Joann admitted that Elizabeth did call her, but explained that they both thought that it would be good for Julia to meet someone since she was still so young and had a long life ahead to think about.

After Julia cooled down a little bit about them "intruding into (her) life," she realized that she should at least think about it. Joann helped her realize that the kids really did need to have someone they could depend upon as a father, and she really needed a husband. Joann told her about a friend of Sonny's who had lost his wife a few years back, and he had no children. Chris was two years older than Julia and worked as an architect. He had come to church where Joann and Sonny went when his wife was still alive. She died suddenly at home, and the medical examiner never did determine the cause of death, although Joann and Sonny weren't privy to that information. Chris seemed to be someone that Julia could trust, and Joann thought that they would be a great match.

After Julia's consent, Joann asked Sonny to get in touch with Chris, and they set up a dinner meeting at their house. Chris was told that there would be someone there that they wanted him to meet, and he seemed quite eager. Chris had seen some other ladies since his wife died, but not anyone that he dated very long or really liked much. Sonny told Chris a good bit about Julia and really hoped that they would hit things off better. Chris had wanted children with his first wife and still did. The fact that Julia had two children made her even more appealing to him.

After Chris heard more about Julia, he decided that he had to figure out the best way of getting to know her better. The idea of a dinner at Sonny's to get them together seemed to be a good idea. They decided that they would set up a time on the next Saturday night for them all to get together and cook supper. Joann contacted Julia and told her of the arrangements.

Julia felt so nervous. It was as though she had to get accustomed to dating again. That queasy feeling was in her stomach, and she spent extraordinary amounts of time in the bathroom that she had not done before. She thought about that and felt like it was so silly of her to be worrying so much about just meeting someone, but she knew it was different. This was someone, whether she realized it or not, that she would measure against Frank, Sr., and someone who would have to be a good father to Frank, Jr., and Sarah. Julia really took seriously the notion of even meeting someone that she might date because that would be someone that she might marry later. That would be someone with whom she would share her deepest secrets and someone who would see her at her best and her worst. That would also be someone who would have a lot of responsibility with the children; it had to be someone whom she could trust. Yes, this small decision to meet Chris was a weighty one indeed.

Elizabeth wanted Julia to allow her to keep Frank and Sarah that Saturday night, but Julia told her that she wanted them to go over to Joann's house so that Chris could meet them. Elizabeth tried to explain that it was important that Julia get to know Chris first, but Julia told her the children were just as important and that Chris had to "like all of us or none of us." Julia remembered the problems that Frank, Sr., had when they first got married, and she wanted to be sure to find someone that she wouldn't have to be the strong one for again. She wanted someone that she could depend upon to be there. Someone that could make her feel secure—that is what she wanted.

Julia spent a couple of hours getting her and the kids ready to go over to Joann and Sonny's. She wanted them to look their best and certainly she wanted to look the best that she could. When they arrived, it was just getting dark that night and Julia really liked the way that they had put landscape lighting around their house. Julia thought to herself how nice it would be to have a house for her and the kids. She thought about how it would feel to have a real family again. Would she have a house one day that would be lit up like that? More than having that, she wanted to have her heart lit up and glowing warmly with someone who would love her as much as she would love him. As she was walking down the sidewalk, the front door opened and a man with a big smile on his face slowly walked out. "He must be Chris," she thought.

He had black hair that was just perfectly combed over to the left with soft facial features, a light complexion, and big, brownish-green eyes. Julia noticed that when he walked, he made slow, sure steps and walked in a very self confident manner. He spoke to her in a soft-spoken, but assertive manner that made Julia almost melt. She had heard the words, "Hello, how are you doing?" at least a thousand times, but it sounded so much better coming from him. Julia didn't realize how much she missed having the companionship of someone that loved her until she saw Chris. Julia didn't know what to say.

"I'm Chris. You must be Julia. Are you okay?"

Julia was so nervous that she was just stammering out whatever came into her mind. "Yes, that's me. I'm Julia. I'm okay. It's nice weather tonight. Don't you think so? Oh, I'm so sorry. Are you okay? Oh, that sounds too trite. I should say more than 'I'm okay.' I'm feeling very well tonight and I'm so glad to get to meet you." She gave him a really big smile realizing that she needed to quit saying whatever she thought before she embarrassed herself further.

Chris could tell that she was trying too hard to be the right kind of person to him. He picked up on that really quickly. Sonny had told him about her children, how young they were, and how they needed a father. Chris thought to himself, "*Hmm, she really needs someone.*" He told her, "I'm so glad and it is an honor to finally meet you. I've heard so much about you. Sonny told me that you have two children. They are not with you tonight?"

Julia apologetically replied as she turned back around and headed toward the car, "Oh, yes, Frank and Sarah are still in the car. I would love for you to meet them. I saw you coming out and wanted to greet you before I brought them inside."

"Well, I would love to meet your children. How old are they? Tell me about them." Chris tried to act as interested as he could, but on the inside he really didn't want to talk about the children. They talked for a little while in front of the house, and Julia told Chris quite a bit about them. She was so proud of them and they meant everything to her. Frank and Sarah didn't seem too excited to meet Chris, however. Something to them just didn't seem right. When Julia went over to the car to get them out, Frank started whining and resisted so much that she had to pull him out of the car. Sarah came a little more willingly, but she knew after watching Frank that she had no choice.

"Chris, this is Frank and the little one is Sarah," Julia introduced while she was still out of breath from struggling with them. "Frank doesn't feel really well and he's just a little cranky. Frank, why don't you shake Mr. Chris' hand?" Frank extended his hand as though he was afraid it was going to be bitten at any moment. Chris knelt down and shook his hand.

"Frank, I'm glad to meet you. You're the man of the house, aren't you?" Chris was trying to make him feel better, but that wasn't the way Frank perceived that question.

"I surely am, and you better not hurt my mommy," Frank declared as he stood straight up with his chest out like a rooster provoked. Chris forced himself to smile and didn't know what to say at first.

"Frank, I would never hurt your mom and I wouldn't even think of bothering you or Sarah either. Your mom brought you over here so we could have some fun. What do you think? Do you want to have some fun tonight?" Chris tried to make Frank feel better the best way he could think.

Frank said "Okay" really slowly as he could tell that he would have to go along with this. He still didn't like this, but he decided that he would make the best of it. Frank grabbed Sarah's hand and they took off to the front door of Sonny's and Joann's house with Julia and Chris following close behind. Chris looked over at Julia and smiled as if he thought he had handled that situation well. Julia wasn't thinking about the words that Chris had used, how Frank had reacted to Chris, or really thinking too much at all except for noticing how handsome Chris' smile looked to her.

When Sonny opened the front door the kids piled in like they were running from a fire. Julia made them come back to the door and walk inside in a more appropriate manner; she apologized for their eagerness. Sonny knew that they hadn't been to other folks' houses too much and understood that they needed the attention. The house had that wonderful back yard barbeque smell as the smoke eased its way in the open back patio door from where they were cooking. Chris went with Sonny to help with the barbequing, and Julia went to the kitchen with the kids to help Joann.

Chris asked Sonny a lot of questions while they were barbecuing to get as much information as possible about Julia. Sonny told him everything that he knew that might help him get to know her better. Julia was just head over heels in how she described to Joann her first reaction to meeting Chris. Joann could certainly tell that it wouldn't be hard to get Julia to agree to go out on a date sometime with Chris. Later that night, Chris did ask her if she would go out with him the next weekend. They were all sitting around the table finishing up their meal, including the children, and Julia hardly gave a second thought before agreeing to let Frank and Sarah stay with Joann that night. Frank and Sarah were not very happy and didn't understand why they weren't the first to be consulted about this.

The next weekend came quickly and Julia had a great time out with Chris. He took her to her favorite restaurant in town. Chris just seemed perfect to her and she couldn't believe that he liked so many of the same things that she did. He even told her how much he had missed being in church and invited her to come to church with him that Sunday. Julia was a little nervous about how quickly things seemed to move, but didn't let it bother her too much. While at church Sunday, Julia loved the thought of all of them together there because it made her feel like the family was more complete again.

That Sunday afternoon, Julia and Chris had some time to talk. He told her about how much he enjoyed spending time with her, and that he hoped the kids would be able to get to know him better. He made plans for him and Julia to get together again soon, and they kept seeing each other for several months. Chris spent time with Sarah and Frank, too, and gained at least their partial trust. He took them to their favorite places to eat and even took them camping with Julia one weekend.

It wasn't long before Chris proposed to Julia, and they were married at a friend's house rather than in a church as Julia had wanted. Julia didn't say anything about it because it seemed like a small matter, and she wanted to make this work for her and the kids. She didn't realize that this was just the beginning of a long list of her wants that would go unfulfilled.

CHAPTER TWELVE

Tying a Tight Knot

Chris' work as an architect had been his life for many years, and he spent most of his time with that activity. Even prior to his first wife's death, he devoted his time to his work, hoping to gain more recognition for the designs he created. Although he spent a lot of time with Julia and the kids prior to the wedding, he didn't spend much time with them afterwards and didn't even attend church as regularly anymore. It was as though he was a different person than who she thought she had married.

Julia hated to have to admit to Joann that they were having problems, but finally broke down and discussed their problems while they were having coffee together one afternoon. Joann told her that Sonny had noticed, too, that Chris hadn't been coming to church, but just figured it was due to his work overloading him. Julia felt as though she was just someone to meet his needs, because he didn't even try to meet her, or the children's, needs anymore. Joann tried to console her the best that she could, but praying for all of them was really what would help them the most.

Frank really needed a father figure in his life, but Chris

certainly ended up being much less than what Julia had anticipated. Frank noticed how upset his mother seemed and told his grandmother about how they were being treated. Julia, of course, was the first to hear about what Frank had told her. She was especially upset about her mother knowing that the marriage wasn't what she portrayed it to be. Julia made attempts to talk to Chris about their relationship and how it bothered Frank. Chris didn't say a whole lot and actually seemed irritated that Frank was not happy.

Frank was outside the house planting some flowers that his mother wanted in a new, little garden they had made. It was a few days later, but Chris still had it in his mind that Frank was just trying to cause them problems in their marriage because he never liked Chris in the beginning. Chris noticed that no one else was around in the backyard and decided that he would confront Frank about what he had said to his grandmother. Frank certainly hadn't planned on being physically challenged by his step-father and could tell that Chris was terribly upset. Chris cornered Frank next to the outside wall where he was working and lifted him up the wall by the neck to tell him, "I know that you are conspiring against me, and you better watch out what you say from now on because I'm going to be watching you."

Frank didn't know what to say in the fear that gripped him at that moment, like the devil himself had wrapped his hand around his neck. He certainly didn't want to be provoking and meekly replied in his tears, "Yes, sir." Frank became reclusive after that and didn't want to tell Julia or anyone much about how Chris was treating him because he was afraid of retribution. Frank tried his best to stay away from Chris as much as possible.

Little Sarah was also affected by Chris' behavior. Chris did seem to like her better initially because he didn't feel threatened by her. He spent more time with Sarah and took her to town for ice cream a lot while Frank stayed home in his room, or went riding on his bike with his friends. Julia had noticed how much time that Chris spent with Sarah, but didn't think anything more of it than most mothers who trust their husbands would. Julia did get concerned, however, when she started noticing the same withdrawn behavior in Sarah that she was noticing in Frank. Sarah wouldn't tell her mom what was bothering her and started staying in her room as much as Frank was staying in his room. Their family didn't communicate anything like they used to before the marriage.

Julia and Chris' time together started to slowly decrease as Chris didn't seem to be interested in Julia at all like he seemed to be before they were married. Chris did make a lot of time for Sarah, however, and tried to find ways frequently that he could get her away from Julia and Frank. While taking Sarah to different places, he often would stop on the side of the road and talk to her about how much he loved her and that they had a special relationship. Chris told her that she couldn't tell anyone about what they talked about because it was their "secret." Chris told Sarah that Julia would not be happy with her if she told Julia anything about how he put his hands on her legs and rubbed them while telling her not to be afraid of him. Chris eventually made Sarah believe that their "special time" together was what all dads did. Sarah didn't know any better and reluctantly believed the one who her mother trusted enough to marry.

After several weeks, Chris had some pictures that he had drawn to show Sarah how they needed "to get to know each other more." Sarah was even more reluctant, but wanted Chris to be happy with her after he told her that he would have to tell Julia how bad she was behaving. Chris would caress her at first, but later he got her to get comfortable with his "game" where they had to touch each other in that "special place." After several months, Chris got Sarah to accept that they had to let their "special places be together" and started having sex with her about once a week. During that time, Sarah was becoming very withdrawn and actually was mad with Julia. Sarah was conditioned to think that she was supposed to do these things and that Julia would be upset with her if she didn't do them. Naturally, she started to have a lot of disruptive and disobedient behavior that many people noticed.

One day Sarah started feeling sick and told her mom that she had a "stomach ache." It wasn't usual for Sarah to feel sick and Julia was already quite concerned about how Sarah had been acting anyway. Julia decided to take Sarah to the doctor after two days of the same complaints. Chris kept telling Julia that it was probably just a virus and it would be gone soon. He didn't want her to take Sarah to the doctor, but Julia did so anyway. While they were there, the doctor could tell that something was bothering Sarah because her weight had decreased since she had been in there for the last visit. Also, she just didn't act like the same happy child that he was accustomed to seeing. Focusing intently on figuring out what was actually happening, the good doctor asked a lot of questions of Sarah after he didn't see a lot wrong with her following a limited, brief exam. Since he couldn't get her to give any more details and couldn't find anything specific, he told Julia to bring her back in if anything changed, or if she didn't get to feeling better.

When they got back home, Chris seemed overly interested to know the details of what the doctor had told Julia and how he had examined Sarah. Julia was really starting to get worried about Sarah and started watching Chris very closely. She decided that she would follow them one day when they went out together on one of their trips "to get ice cream." Julia knew where the ice cream shop was located that he said they went to visit, but she noticed he took a different road and ended up on this small dirt road next to an old, abandoned house.

Julia had been following from a long distance so that Chris wouldn't notice her. She parked her car at the beginning of the dirt road and walked the rest of the quarter of a mile until she saw the old house. Julia just couldn't understand why in the world they would be going to such a deserted place and, although she had wondered why they spent so much time together, she had brushed aside any worrisome concerns. She thought maybe the kids just needed more time to adjust to Chris.

Walking quietly up to the old house, she could hear them talking inside. She went to an outside wall where there were some loose boards so she could see inside. When she looked inside, she saw Chris partially clothed while Sarah was completely undressed. Julia was aghast as she saw Chris touching Sarah in a way that no one should touch a child. Sarah started whimpering and then crying like she usually did. Julia was enraged as any mother would have been. Not even thinking of herself, she screamed as loudly as she could and ran around to the front door of the house. Chris was surprised, but could think of nothing except how he could conceal what Julia had seen. He hollered loud enough for Julia to hear him, "It's not what you think," as he frantically was trying to put on his clothes and threw Sarah's clothes over on her. Julia knew that there was no good explanation for what she had seen. She found a solid 4x4 outside and broke down the flimsy front door in a matter of seconds.

What Julia didn't know was that Chris actually owned that old house and had been using it for this purpose for several years even before they had met. Julia also didn't know that Chris had been almost discovered by his first wife, but he poisoned her with a drug that made her have a heart attack. Chris kept a gun hidden in the old house. He knew that if Julia left there he surely would be in a lot of trouble. He pushed Sarah to the back of the front room where they were and, as Julia came bursting through the front door, shot Julia three times right in front of Sarah. All that Julia could do was to look up into Sarah's eyes as she prayed that God would rescue her somehow from Chris. That vision was one that Sarah would never forget along with all of the other trauma before, and to come.

All Sarah could do was cry as she curled herself up in the corner of the dark, big room. Chris told her that if she moved, she would "get it next." He went around to the back of the house and dragged Julia out to the woods where he buried her in a deep hole that he had already dug before just in case something like this ever came up. He had some bleach and cleaned up the entire front of the house where he had shot her. Sarah was still in the corner, shaking and almost in shock. Chris knew that he would never be able to explain what had happened to Julia and decided that the best thing to do was to take Sarah with him and leave as soon as possible. He tied Sarah up and taped up her mouth with duct tape so that she wouldn't be found until he could get back.

Chris left and went to their house to get together most of his clothes along with some of Sarah's clothes, some food, and other items before going to the bank and withdrawing all of their money. Before he could leave the house, Frank came into the bedroom where Chris was packing and asked him where he was going. Chris told him, "I don't want to be married to your mother anymore and I don't like you either. I'm leaving. You can go to your grandfather's house."

Frank wasn't one to back away too easily and asked Chris, "Where is Sarah? Is she with you? She's been acting really funny here lately. What have you done with her?" Frank's voice got louder and more urgent as he spoke each sentence, like he was starting to understand that there was more here than just Chris wanting to leave them. Frank also knew how Chris had treated him in the past and wasn't about to stay around after he had spoken. Frank knew he couldn't overpower Chris and had better get out of there as quickly as he could. He was backing up as he asked his last question; then he turned and ran for the door.

Chris knew that he needed some time to be able to get out of the area and certainly didn't need Frank leaving right then to tell the authorities. He ran after him and caught him just before Frank was able to get to the door. Frank was hollering at him to leave him alone and to let him go, but Chris knew he had to silence him. After he pinned Frank down to the floor, he hit him in the head with a large iron skillet and then got some nylon string from a kitchen drawer above where they fought and tied his hands behind his back before taping his mouth with duct tape.

Chris certainly hadn't planned on encountering Frank like this and wasn't sure what to do with Frank. He finally decided that he had to kill him, or he'd never get very far before Frank would tell on him. Frank was still unconscious from being hit in the head, so Chris got a large suitcase and curled Frank up in it. He carried all of the luggage out to the car and went back to the old house after going by the bank. The teller at the bank noticed how nervous and impatient Chris was acting while he was in the drive through waiting.

Chris got the suitcase that Frank was in and carried it out behind the house where Julia was. Frank was starting to awaken and was pushing and trying to holler by the time he got to the scene of so much terror. This was terror, not from an outside threat, but a terror that had arisen within Chris and now had control of him. Chris had chosen to grant this control slowly and steadily by giving in to all those temptations inside of him. He didn't even think for himself at this point and was just acting upon the impulses of what had control of him.

Chris could only think that he had to silence Frank before he got free so he got the shovel and beat him in the head without even taking him out of the suitcase. Chris dug another hole and threw the suitcase in. He hit Frank a few more times to be sure he was dead and then covered him up. Chris got some leaves from the woods and scattered them over the area where Julia and Frank were to make it look more natural before heading back to the old house.

Sarah was still crouched in the corner and had very red and swollen eyes from crying so much. She had heard the noise from where she was and knew what must have happened. All hope was gone from within her when she realized that no one knew where she was and what was happening. Chris came in the door, picked her up, and threw her over his shoulder like a sack of potatoes, or some other commodity to be used. She certainly couldn't be allowed to be seen in the car traveling with him like she was, so he put her in the trunk for the time being. They were headed out west to San Francisco where he thought he could hide better.

The knot had been tied so tightly that it had broken, because the strings that it was made of were weak and of no substance. The terror within Chris tried to tell him that he had done the right thing and that Frank had it coming to him for a long time anyway. He hated being caught by Julia, but rationalized her killing because he saw it as the only way to hide what he thought was love for Sarah. The misguided and perverted mindset he had didn't develop overnight. Chris had nurtured it and had allowed it to overcome him by making bad choices when temptations faced him. He couldn't turn back now and the terror inside him would almost completely consume him, too, before it was over.

CHAPTER THIRTEEN

The Great Escape

Chris thought he had planned things fairly well for someone who had to come up with an escape plan quickly. His racing mind certainly hadn't covered his tracks as well as he thought, but he set out on his way since he had no choice. He was convinced that he was smart enough to overcome these obstacles that had presented themselves. However, he was not anywhere near in intelligence to the One that Julia prayed to before she died.

While he was driving, he could hear Sarah crying in spite of the duct tape he still had on her mouth. He decided to turn on the radio, but more than really wanting to listen to the radio, he was trying to find something louder than Sarah's cries. He turned to the first station that he could tune in well, and it was a Christian radio station. There was someone talking at that time, and Chris felt a pang within him when he heard the convicting words of a preacher who spoke from John, "*For God so loved the world that He gave His only begotten Son, that whoever believes in Him should not perish but have everlasting life. For God did not send His Son into the world to condemn the world, but that the world through Him might be saved. He who believes in Him is not condemned; but he who does not believe is condemned already, because he has not believed in the name of the only begotten Son of God. And this is the condemnation, that the light has come into the world, and men loved darkness rather than light, because their deeds were evil. For everyone practicing evil hates the light and does not come to the light, lest his deeds should be exposed. But he who does the truth comes to the light, that his deeds may be clearly seen, that they have been done in God*" (John 3:16-21). Chris heard those words and it was as though a light had been directly shown on his deeds. Having a choice at that moment, he chose to follow the same path he was already taking and reacted in outrage, almost tearing the radio out of the car.

Elizabeth, Sarah's great grandmother, hadn't felt well the entire day and she instinctively knew that there had to be something very wrong. She had tried to call their house, but got no answer for a longer time than usual. She decided to drive over and see what was happening. When she pulled up to the house, she felt an eerie quietness about the place. She could see that the car was gone and decided to take a look around. The front door had a window beside it which Elizabeth stooped down to look through and noticed that there was a mess on the floor. This certainly seemed unusual for them. She decided that she better get back over to her house and bring William with her to see if he could help figure out what was going on.

William was outside working on cleaning up some trash someone had thrown out in the yard when Elizabeth came driving up fairly quickly. She hollered over to William from the street to "go get the spare keys to Julia's house" that Julia had given them in case they ever needed them. William had a look of bewilderment on this face, but knew Elizabeth well enough to know that if she was worried, he should be, too.

He ran and got the keys and jumped in the car just quickly enough to get the door closed before she started driving. Elizabeth told him about what she had seen at the house and that she just knew something horrible had to have happened.

When they got to the house and entered through the front door, they first noticed scuff marks on the floor leading up to the door. Then they saw a skillet by the sink with what looked like blood on the base of it opposite the handle. Several drawers in the kitchen were left open as if someone had gone through them very quickly because the contents were all jumbled up and a lot of it was on the floor. They went to the back of the house where Sarah's room was located and found that a lot of her clothes missing from her closet. They found that a lot of Chris' clothes were missing, too, but didn't find the same for Frank or Julia. This was certainly enough for them to decide they needed to call the police immediately and get an investigation started.

After the police had finished doing their work at the house, they told Elizabeth and William that there was obvious evidence of some foul play involved, but it would take further work to figure what had happened. They still had to find out why the whole family had disappeared. There was nothing further that they could do there, but to ask questions and see if anyone else had noticed anything. A neighbor across the street had come and told the police that they had seen Chris take a lot of suitcases out of the house and wondered then where he was going. Elizabeth and William were just beside themselves. They held each other as they slowly walked over to the car and left the scene. When they got back to their house, they knelt and prayed for the Lord to help them find out what had happened and where their family was.

Elizabeth had a hair brush belonging to Frank that he had left at their house one night recently when he had spent the night with them. She took it to the police department for them to run DNA analysis on and compare with the blood specimen found on the skillet at the house. They had checked all of the hospitals in the vicinity and had found no trace of any of them. William went to the local newspaper, radio, and television stations so that features could be run about the missing family. The bank teller remembered Chris coming through to withdraw all of the money from their account and how nervous he was then.

After two weeks, they still had few other leads until the police department called them and confirmed that the DNA on the skillet matched the samples from the brush. Since the neighbor had seen Chris leave with the luggage, he certainly was a suspect, but where were they? And why was there no trace of any of them?

While all of the investigation was ongoing, Chris had grown a beard and lightened his hair color. He cut Sarah's hair a lot shorter and dyed it black. After they had gotten moved into the San Francisco area, Chris felt like they were far enough away where no one could possibly recognize them. He let Sarah come out into the public with him for brief episodes then, but he had threatened her so much that she was too afraid to do anything besides what he told her. Chris got a job at an architectural firm in a suburb of San Francisco after he had gotten a false identity and then a California driver's license. He made up some stories about his past employment and the boss there didn't check out his story since Chris seemed like a decent person. The employer really needed some help with their work load anyway so he decided to leave off the verification that time.

He had gotten Sarah a fake identification card also and had concocted a good sounding story that he made her memorize. It was about where her mother was and Chris made her repeat what he told her until she could quote it perfectly: "She was killed in a car accident with my brother, and only me and daddy lived." Chris wouldn't let her speak of Frank, her real dad, and told her the fake story so much she just about believed it.

Sarah was made to stay at the house all day long with the doors locked and was not allowed to let anyone come inside, or answer the telephone. Chris checked on her at lunch daily to be sure she was there. Every night Sarah was in horror wondering how Chris was going to act when he got there. She had grown so accustomed to his abuse that it seemed like a routine to her after the last two years of putting up with it. Sarah had just turned nine years old at her most recent birthday away from all that she had known and loved. A state of despair had certainly set in to stay for a long time to come.

Chris felt sure that by the time six months had passed since their get away, he would be home free. However, he had no idea of the search that was occurring from where he came. A hunter had been out in the woods with beagles trying to round them up to go home after a day of hunting. In trying to find them, he came upon the old house where Chris had been earlier. One of his beagles was over there sniffing the ground and digging at the site of the graves that Chris had put Julia, and then Frank, into. The hunter went to see what the dogs were so interested in and noticed that the ground had been recently dug there. He then went over to the old house and found evidence that someone had been there recently. Being suspicious as to what was going on at the old house, thought to have been abandoned long ago, he called the sheriff who came out there.

The sheriff had checked the records at the county tax collector's office and discovered that Chris owned the old place. He knew, of course, that the whole family was missing. Sheriff McKenzie had been around for a long time and had a bad feeling about what he was going to find out at that old house. The investigation that ensued concluded that Frank, Jr., and Julia had been murdered. Chris was wanted, not just for questioning now, but was wanted for murder; the authorities did not know what had happened to Sarah, but assumed that she must be with him or was buried somewhere else. They could only guess as to why this all had happened. A nationwide alert for the two missing people was issued and all law enforcement offices around the country were notified to be on the look out for Chris and Sarah.

After the funerals, William and Elizabeth had spent about two weeks being really depressed and questioning God as to why this all had happened. They certainly couldn't understand it and asked Him for guidance in understanding. They also asked for His help in locating Chris and Sarah. The community couldn't have been more supportive of them, especially their church family. When all of this happened, they were in such a state of shock that it took them some time to be able to accept the fact that it wasn't a dream, but was reality. Both William and Elizabeth kept wondering if this really did happen, or if they would awaken soon from this horrible nightmare. Each morning, although, they awoke and had to face the cold, hard fact that Julia and Frank, Jr., were dead. That was hard enough, but the hardest part of it all was wondering exactly how Chris had escaped and whether he had Sarah with him, or if she was buried somewhere else they had yet to discover.

The stage of denial being over, the next stage of grief set in for them both —anger. One of the good things that their anger did for them was to motivate them to get busy trying to find Chris, and hopefully Sarah, too. Chris was smart, but he wasn't smarter than the workings which he couldn't see. He wasn't a match for the prayers of two motivated grandparents of Sarah who were now intent on finding her. It wasn't just them praying either; many folks in their community joined them in calling for help from their Creator. This time of tragedy could have some good outcomes if they kept their faith.

CHAPTER FOURTEEN

The Hunt is On

Chris watched the newspapers regularly and also followed programs on television to see if anything was making its way to their area. He had become very paranoid of anyone at all coming around and felt as though he were being watched all the time. His performance at his job wasn't very good, and his employer wondered what in the world this new man he had hired was doing to be so distracted. Chris didn't even let Sarah go to school for fear of someone learning something about them. He became so engrossed with running from having to face the consequences of his actions that he left Sarah alone more which certainly was good for her.

While Chris was being tormented through what little conscience he had left, William had been contacting media outlets in many different areas to find out how he could get some publicity. He got many publishers to run the story of what had happened and print the pictures of Chris and Sarah with the article. They kept praying that someone who knew Chris would see the pictures. It was a very time-consuming process to try to get this out all over the country. William knew they had to be somewhere still in the country; he felt it. He finally got a national television program to run the story and they even published the pictures with the possible changes in hair color, length, and other variations that would be possible with Chris and Sarah.

Chris was at home the night the program aired, but didn't watch it as he normally did. He had gotten himself a bottle of Vodka so he could forget about himself for a while. One of the other employees at the architectural firm where Chris worked did watch the program, however. Robert recognized Chris right off, but he didn't know him as Chris. Robert called the program's toll-free number listed on the bottom of the screen and gave them some information about Chris. It was not long before the law enforcement officials in California were comparing notes with the sheriff from where Chris came.

They decided that they would put surveillance on Chris initially to see where he lived because they went to the address that his employer had on record and found out that it wasn't his address at all. When the undercover officer followed Chris home on Monday afternoon the next week, he noticed that the house had no open curtains or blinds. The officer knew that Sarah could be inside, or dead, and he decided to watch for a few days, or longer if needed, to see if Chris would lead him to anything.

Chris had started to notice that the other workers at his job were treating him differently. Those different looks that he got and the mutterings when they thought he couldn't hear them were really getting to him. He knew that something was up and began to think that he needed to get Sarah and leave the area just in case he had been found out. After he got off work on Wednesday afternoon, he decided that he needed to go ahead with moving as soon as possible. The place where he was staying was being rented by the month, so it wouldn't be too hard to leave it.

The surveillance officer was kept aware of how Chris was acting at work and noticed that Chris had made several trips to and from the house Wednesday afternoon. He was getting some of the furnishings out of the house and loading them in the car to take them to a storage facility. The officer telephoned his superiors to let them know of Chris' recent actions. They figured that he would be trying to get out of the area so they decided to arrest him while they had him. They hadn't seen Sarah at all, but couldn't wait any longer. After a warrant was delivered along with several back up officers, they made their approach to the house before Chris could leave again.

They surrounded the house on the outside and a small group went to the front door. It was assumed that he would put up a struggle and they had the force necessary to deal with that if necessary. Chris heard the knock on the front door and knew that it certainly wasn't the pizza man coming to pay a visit. He looked out a side window and saw several officers. Chris' mind went into a panic, but he knew that he had been caught. The officers knocked once more and called out to him again, but Chris didn't respond. They knew he was inside, so they got a battering ram and broke down the door to find Chris quietly sitting in a chair in the kitchen with his head down. He didn't even put up a fight and actually seemed a little relieved that he had been caught. Sarah was crouched in a backroom when they found her; she was quite emotionless and didn't know what to think about what was happening. Chris was taken to the county jail while Sarah was taken to a local hospital for evaluation by a primary care physician and a psychiatrist.

William and Elizabeth were notified after Sarah was admitted to the hospital. They were elated that Sarah was alive, but knew that she would need a lot of attention to try to overcome what had happened. They had no idea of the type of abuse that she had endured until the physician told them when they arrived. Chris denied it all, but the evidence was quite clear. After the police got his fingerprints, they matched the ones taken from the skillet and from several areas around the old house.

Chris had a public defender to represent him at the trial. He couldn't explain anything that would back up his denials of the facts. The jury returned a guilty verdict on two counts of second degree murder, one count of kidnapping, and multiple other charges. He was sentenced to life in prison without the possibility of parole. After the trial was over, it made William and Elizabeth feel better to know that they wouldn't have to publicly go over all of it again, but the hurt certainly remained. No punishment that could be meted out to Chris would take that away.

CHAPTER FIFTEEN

A Time of Recovery

Little Sarah was just pitiful. She was receiving counseling which was helping some, but she remained very withdrawn. Her family had to practically force her involvement with them to keep her from isolating herself completely. Sarah lived in her own world much of the time and didn't invite people into it because that certainly helped her to feel unthreatened. The counselor tried to help her by role playing with dolls so that Sarah could express some of her emotions held inside her.

William and Elizabeth knew that the best thing that they could do was to show Sarah unconditional love and a lot of attention. They also prayed for her daily that the Lord would heal her in His time. They took her to church regularly and she enjoyed going to Sunday School with the other kids a lot. She sang with the other children and, looking at her during those times, one wouldn't know all that really troubled her. A time of singing to occupy her mind's thoughts was just the therapy she needed and was one good way for her to express her feelings.

The teacher talked one day about prayer and how

important that it is. Sarah remembered how she had heard Julia pray and how she was taught to pray a simple prayer at bedtime. She still prayed that prayer every night at her great-grandparents, but her prayer had changed. Her prayer became different during the time that she was held against her will by Chris. During those times when she was locked up inside that house, she would crouch in the corner as if to feel safer by having two walls on each side of her where no one could come up from behind. Her prayer was more than the usual "Now I lay me down to sleep…" Sarah prayed for safety; she prayed for a refuge from this trouble. She didn't know what to pray for more specifically, but she knew to Whom she was praying. The only time that she felt safe was when she was praying and felt His presence there with her. He had provided a refuge for her during those times. When she was rescued, Sarah was so thankful to Him for answering her prayer, and Julia's prayer, that she could hardly put it into words. She knew then that He must have known her heart's cry.

Sarah told the teacher after the class that day about how she had prayed during that time and how He had answered her prayer. The teacher, Jewel, held back her tears as she knew what Sarah had just gone through. Why had she been allowed to be the victim of such evil? Jewel explained to Sarah that God loves us so much that He lets us make our own choices. He doesn't force us to love Him or to obey Him. Some people choose to do evil in spite of the knowledge in their hearts that what they are doing is wrong. Good people do suffer, but the difference is that God will bring something good out of something intended for bad. Jewel told Sarah that He would always be there for her and that she could always trust Him.

In William and Elizabeth's neighborhood, Sarah slowly got to where she would go outside more. She ventured away from the house, under watchful eyes, during the afternoon time when school was out for the day. Sarah met several of the local kids in the area as she walked down the sidewalks near their houses. One of them was Angie, a little red-headed girl, who saw Sarah walking alone with her head down kicking rocks off the sidewalk. Angie ran over and kicked one of the rocks back from the road toward the side-walk where Sarah was walking.

Sarah looked up to see who had just kicked that rock back and was messing up her sidewalk cleaning effort. When she saw her, Angie was leaning over with her hands on her knees and looking up toward Sarah with a big smile. Sarah's big frown quickly transformed into a smile, too, and Angie ran over to introduce herself. They hit it off great together, and Angie was just the friend that Sarah had been needing. Days after school were filled with times of games, dolls, and playing house while the weekends consisted of plenty of sleep-overs. Sarah really began to express herself, and, to a small degree, she was coming out of the hard shell that she had formed out of necessity. The more that she got to know Angie, the more she showed her true self who most people weren't familiar with at all.

There was another one of her classmates that liked Sarah and tried his best to get a smile out of her every day. Patrick would sneak up behind Sarah and pull her pig tail before running off while she hollered at him. Sarah knew he was just picking with her and even though she acted like she didn't like it, she really did like the attention that she was getting. Patrick would sit across the lunch room and stare at Sarah sometimes until she would look at him when he would make an ugly face. Sarah would make an ugly face back and then hold her head down before he could do it again. They both enjoyed picking on each other.

Angie talked her parents into getting her a "doll house" and putting it outside behind their house. She and Sarah would go out there and spend hours role playing; sometimes they would get their sleeping bags and spend all night playing, talking, listening to their favorite music, making various food dishes, and pretending to keep house. Angie's mom would go out and check on them occasionally to be sure they hadn't got into some trouble. Seeing them reminded her of when she was growing up; it seemed like a good while back, but then again it seemed like yesterday.

Sarah did really well in her school work and got awards regularly. She was really quiet most of the time, and the majority of the other kids misunderstood her quiet demeanor. In her own mind, she wanted to be outgoing and expressive, but something held her back and wouldn't let her be the person that she wanted to be. She felt uneasy during those situations and would resort to what had always worked for her before. Sarah knew that she could hide within herself to feel safe and secure. She figured that she wouldn't get hurt if she didn't reach out. She was an excellent thinker and felt secure by doing her best in her school work. Pouring her all into her studies was one sure and safe way of accomplishing something worthy of the praise and reassurance that she needed.

There was something missing deep on the inside of her that she could tell wasn't right. She tried to ignore that fact as much as she could by staying busy. Her folks could tell that she was restless, but all that they actually knew to do was to pray for her and show her the unconditional love she needed. In doing that, they knew that they would be modeling God's love to her and would help her to one day understand Him better.

Her Sunday School teachers were a big help to her, too, and they spent as much time with her as possible. They knew that if she was taught while she was a child what she needed to know and brought up in the ways of God, she would not depart from it when she was older.

At the church she attended, they had a yearly camp that

all the children attended each summer. Sarah and Angie went together each year from the time they were eleven years old. That was another source of healing for Sarah. All the children that went to the camp knew that they were valued highly. The various activities that they did reinforced what they were taught through listening. Sarah didn't understand it at that time, but those years of learning gave her knowledge of the Bible that would help to save her life, physically and spiritually.

One day after Sarah had gotten back from church, her great-grandparents had prepared the usual, wonderful Sunday meal which they all enjoyed and then retired to the living room to talk and just spend time together. Sarah always loved to spend time reading and writing. She had seemed a little troubled that day during the message she heard from the pastor, but no one thought too much about her demeanor because she was normally relatively quiet. Sarah was growing into her early teenage years and attended the regular worship service with all of the other adults. While Sarah was sitting on the couch she wrote a poem that afternoon:

I was sitting in church today;
My heavy burden I did carry.
He told that there is a better way—
"Release that load here to bury."
But I'm used to carrying it alone,
I want my load on my back to remain.
What could I do except maybe to loan.
"Give Me that load to take away the drain."
I don't know. I'm so used to wearing
That weight without, it would be so light.
"Give Me that load that you've been bearing,
And your future will be so much more bright."
I'll give it to You for a season,

But remember I want it back.
Guilt for not carrying it—that is the reason.
That load without—I would not know how to act.
The vision I saw was one of him—it's him!
The one I barely knew, but miss him still.
An arm around me he placed to go meet Him.
"Release this burden — it's His will."
That embrace felt so warm, so real!
It was usually Him, but now it was Him and him.
I wanted it to stay, but with life I must deal.
Keep your eyes closed so you can see them.
"Let go of the hurt — it's time you really live.
Carry this no more — put it on Him, my Father.
Leave it there this time after you give."
Without the hurt I can remember him, my father.

Sarah was obviously learning some valuable lessons and when she gave the poem to William and Elizabeth, they both rejoiced and praised God for His intervention in Sarah's life. The poem revealed that Sarah knew what she needed to do, but it didn't point to a decision having been made. Their prayers and time had been worth it all to see her growing up with such an insight. They were getting old and never had expected they would have to help raise their great-grandchild. They knew that getting Sarah to the point of releasing that burden would require more sacrifice, and it had been tough on them all, but times like this made it clear that their sacrifices were worth it and more.

Another relationship that needed mending in Sarah's life was her relationship with her grandparents, Cecil and Susan. Neither of them had had much to do with Julia since the time they became disappointed with her when she got involved with Frank. They had let that disappointment turn into an angry grudge and an unforgiving spirit, not realizing that they really needed forgiveness themselves.

The Holy Spirit had never let them rest concerning their relationship they had with their daughter, and they had been especially troubled after the tragedy of her murder. The time that they wished they had spent with Julia had left them. Cecil and Susan had let that drive them apart; they both grieved privately instead of sharing the hurt with one another, or even their church or friends. Many lunch breaks came when one could find Cecil having taken the time to venture out to the cemetery and talk to his daughter at the grave——talking to her now when he could only wish she could talk back. Susan had the same practice about once a week.

Sarah had gotten old enough to drive and she, too, went out to visit with her mother and brother at the cemetery. She had gone there to that place many times before. Sometimes she would go and just sit there, hoping to feel something that would help her to sense closeness to those who seemed so far away. To have just one conversation again, to have just one hug again, to be told "I love you" and "I'm here for you" were words that she dreamed she would hear, but knew that it was impossible. Sarah took a candle out there one night when she couldn't sleep and sat on the ground for an hour looking at that monument with its deep, sharp etchings; she poured out her heart and just hoped that someone heard her cries for understanding and for the love of parents now lost. Placing her hand on the shiny, front surface of the stone monument was like placing her hand on a thick, dividing glass that she just hoped someone from the other side would place their hand onto so she could at least feel the warmth of their touch. She longed to even feel the slightest hint that someone was there, but all that she felt was coldness.

One day when she was walking through the vast array of those cold stones, Sarah saw both Cecil and Susan at that hallowed site. She paused for a moment as she was unsure what to say to her grandparents who hadn't had much to do with her. Sarah didn't know it, but Cecil was the first one that had come that day. Susan had encountered him after she had decided to make a visit that day, too. After each of them saw that the other felt the same way, it certainly opened a door to talking about the subject. They had just said to each other that they wished they had done a lot of things differently and that they would like to have an opportunity to make it as right as possible. Right after voicing that sentiment to one another, here came Sarah walking toward them. The choice was theirs to take this very obvious opportunity that they were being handed on a silver platter and make the best of it, or turn more bitter and cold. Cecil looked at Susan as if to say that there had been enough of this hurt for them all. His look toward her was one that conveyed more meaning than any group of words could ever portray. Susan, in a split second, knew what Cecil felt because she felt it, too. They both felt that inner desire for peace that comes through forgiveness from Him and for others. This was a chance right in front of them to make the right decision and help Sarah, and themselves, heal through Him.

Sarah kept walking down the gently sloping hill toward them, but was very slow and awkward in her approach. She wasn't sure if she was wanted there and looked into their eyes for some sign of acceptance. Cecil and Susan both had made their decision as to how they would react. They both gently smiled as they knelt down and extended their arms open wide! Sarah was left with no doubt that there had been a change of heart with both of them. She ran to them at that point and what a reunion they had right there next to Julia, Frank, and Frank, Jr.'s graves. They left that day with a renewed commitment to mending their relationships and seeking Him more earnestly.

Susan called Elizabeth later that day, and they all got together the next Sunday for lunch. It was feeling a little like home again to them all. A split second decision for each of them between what they knew in their hearts was right and what they were tempted to do in selfishness and pride had made the difference. Having been obedient to what they knew was His guidance, their prayers weren't hindered and even the prayer before their meal that day really felt like they were sitting right there with Him—thanking Him, worshipping His greatness, His patience, His long-suffering, His grace. He was there with them and He was pleased.

Sarah's grandparents and great-grandparents could easily tell the impact of all the traumatic experiences upon Sarah's life so far. Having the family reunited was wonderful and helpful, but healing all the damage that had been done would require a remedy that none of them knew where to find except in Him. Susan and Cecil spent more time with Sarah trying to get to know her better and offering what advice they could on how to cope with her conflicting emotions. They tried to get Sarah to see a counselor, but she didn't want to go. She told them that she just didn't want to talk about anything. The only person that Sarah would discuss much about how she really felt about matters was Angie.

It wasn't long before both Sarah and Angie were old enough to start dating. Angie dated a few different boys in their class at school, but Sarah didn't date anyone. Sarah couldn't bring herself to let anyone get too close to her and certainly didn't want to have to deal with those emotions she had bottled up. The emotions that enslaved her were the result of the loss of that relationship with her real father, Frank, and then the abuse she had endured from Chris. Chris was supposed to have protected her and was supposed to have been the father to her that she had lost. Instead, he raped her, took advantage of her innocence, and was anything but a father to her. Chris was in a prison in California and Sarah was in a prison of her own making. Chris was locked up to keep him from hurting someone else. Sarah was locked up to keep anyone from hurting her. Breaking the chains that bound her would take time and much more.

Sarah still spent most of her time reading and doing activities that were introspective in nature. She continued to outperform most of her classmates in her school work. Something that she didn't do was attending social functions very much. Sarah didn't even go to her high school dances each year. There again, she wanted to go and be a part of activities, but something made her feel uneasy and unaccepted. Sarah would usually come up with some reason why she was too busy too attend. She would spend time studying or working. Everyone who thought they knew her said that she would be able to do anything that she wanted to do with her life.

In her heart, Sarah just wanted to feel like a normal person along with everyone else. She wanted to feel like she was a part of what others enjoyed doing, but that hard shell around her was too hard for even her to break. Sarah found it so difficult to relate to her other classmates that she just gave up on trying to do so. Angie, however, made it a point to reach out to Sarah and wanted her friendship. The attention that Angie showed was so cherished by Sarah, but Sarah was a friend to her only as long as she felt in control. She still wanted to be sure not to be vulnerable. Developing a trust of others again would take a long time, if it ever did.

CHAPTER SIXTEEN

Getting on with Life

It wasn't long before Sarah was graduating from high school and looking forward to what she hoped would be a new beginning to something better. She had talked with a counselor at the local community college while still in high school about her choices of what she wanted to do with her life. Sarah decided that she wanted to become a psychologist so that she could help other people deal with similar problems in life that she had experienced. What Sarah didn't understand was that her decision to become a psychologist also had a lot to do with the fact that she really wanted to understand herself better. She didn't know it at the time, but this was therapy for her as much as it would be for those with whom she counseled as a psychologist.

One of the science instructors at the college and also helped with student counseling regarding course choices. She had directed Sarah to the right courses to take for the first two years so that she could complete the basics for a liberal arts degree before transferring to a university. Sarah enjoyed the new material that she was learning. It was exciting to her to have all of those new insights brought before her on a routine basis at the college. She went through all of the required courses with ease, but the ones that were related to psychology she found especially interesting.

The new ways of thinking about various topics was good for her, but it was also troubling. Having to read about issues that were even remotely related to her past experiences really stirred her emotions. The fire of torment within her was rekindled by having to deal with those issues and Sarah certainly felt the burning within herself.

She would learn later, although, that the same fire would bring the dross to the surface to be skimmed off and a much purer gold would remain. The ashes of what was burned off, that lay at her feet, were those of what she thought she had needed, but didn't. Sarah felt other times like she was being beat around like a tree she would see in the front yard when high winds came through. The same wind that tossed the tree of her life back and forth also served to strengthen it more for the next time that strong winds would come.

Learning how to deal with the emotions within herself would take her some time to understand. Sarah continued trying to deal with the issues within by attempting to understand herself solely from a human psychological viewpoint. Even though she acknowledged God and recognized His guidance in her life thus far, she still did not have a close enough relationship with Him to understand that true and complete healing for her life would only come through Him.

Her friend, Angie, had moved off to a different city to attend a large university. They corresponded by letters frequently and talked on the telephone quite a bit. About twice a year they would get to see each other during the holiday season and at summer. Angie was enjoying being away from home; she was dating different people and getting really involved in a lot of different activities on her campus. Angie tried to get Sarah to come to where she was attending because she thought it would be good for her, but

Sarah wanted to remain where she was. It was close to home and something about that made her feel better.

The new experiences changed them both as they were maturing intellectually. Having to think about life's great questions and come to some understanding was indeed challenging when the teachings of the Christian faith conflicted with what was being taught. Both of them tried to find ways to make their faith consistent with the science of the day. They didn't initially realize that they were making a mistake. Later, they understood that the science of the day should have been understood from a viewpoint of their faith. Sarah had made up her mind that there was no middle ground when it came to the origins of life question. She firmly believed in what she was taught from Genesis and didn't try to make evolution fit into her faith. After researching the issue herself, she learned that there was more evidence for a created universe than for any other theory being discussed. Angie and Sarah encouraged each other on topics such as this when they got to visit.

Sarah worked some on the side while attending college. She had gotten a job at a local grocery store as a cashier and worked nights and weekends usually. Being out in the public was good for her because it helped her to learn how to interact with others and to see how different people lived their lives. Every contact that she had was a small lesson about something. All of the information that her mind took in would certainly affect what she would become.

Sarah thought about her dad, Frank, when she was at the store working. She thought about how he had been working to make something better for his family. Frank's background hadn't been the best in the world and he had made some mistakes, but he eventually did straighten out to be very responsible before his tragic death. Once in a while, Sarah would talk to someone who remembered her dad. When she heard how they would describe his trustworthiness and his good work habits, it made her feel proud and want to be the same kind of example when she worked.

Sarah was in contact with her grandparents quite often to let them know how she was faring while in school. Cecil and Susan had developed so much more of a love for Sarah since they had met in the cemetery that day. They had some time to think and reflect on matters while the Holy Spirit dealt with them, too. What resulted was a wonderful relationship which was what Sarah had needed. Susan came to visit Sarah at least once a week and tried to encourage her. The support that she had now with Susan and Elizabeth was invaluable to her and would help her tremendously.

Sarah graduated from community college with honors and was able to get a scholarship to attend one of the state universities which was about two hours driving time from home. Elizabeth had applied for a scholarship for Sarah to be able to attend. What a surprise it was to everyone else for Elizabeth hadn't told anyone that she had sent in the application. Her time at the community college had ended that May and they all knew that living arrangements would have to be decided upon for her to move to the university in August. Elizabeth, Susan, and Sarah traveled together one weekend to the campus and found an apartment that would be affordable for Sarah if she worked part-time while attending there. Sarah moved in that weekend with the few possessions that she owned.

Sarah was so excited about becoming more independent, but was also afraid of what would lie ahead. Saying goodbye to Susan and Elizabeth was difficult for Sarah and for them. They all knew that a milestone in her life had just occurred and that Sarah would never be a permanent resident of their homes again. Both Susan and Elizabeth reflected on memories of when they had each left home for a new phase of life. Each of them thought about all of the good and bad times that had occurred since that time. They both knew of how difficult it was to start out on their own. They also knew that Sarah was strong enough not to just be able to handle it, but to excel in this new life ahead. All of those thoughts went through their minds as they gave each other a hug while saying parting words at the car outside of her apartment. The initial sadness of leaving Sarah turned to gladness because they were able to see her get to this point in her life. Susan certainly had her regrets for the time that was missed in their relationship, but still felt proud that they had a good relationship now.

This was another time for Sarah's life to be molded further into the person that God wanted her to be, even though Sarah didn't always understand that fact. Elizabeth and Susan understood that concept and it was evident to them that the Lord had His hand upon her life. In those parting moments, as they realized those thoughts, they felt confident that Sarah was going to be just fine. She couldn't be in better hands.

After they left, Sarah went back inside and started arranging her books and other possessions in her apartment. She got things situated like she wanted them and then left to go to the grocery store. This was the first time that she had ever gone to buy food just for herself. She didn't have to get anything that she didn't want to buy and could eat whatever she wanted. What a temptation it was! Probably the best thing that helped her to eat what she needed, and not what she wanted, was the cost. She knew that she had a certain amount of money that had to last the entire semester, so she figured out on a monthly basis what her budget had to stay under. Sarah got so tired of eating ramen noodles that she vowed she'd never eat them again as soon as she could afford something better.

Her first classes were starting on the next Monday and that left her with four days to get to know her way around the campus. After roaming around campus for the first day,

Sarah decided that she would drive around the area outside of the campus to see what there would be to do when she had leisure time. There was a bowling alley on the main road through town and not much else except for several bars in the downtown area. Sarah didn't care for any of that. One attraction that she really liked was the national park that was about ten miles down the nearby highway. That park was just the place she needed when she could go there. A gigantic lake surrounded by nature trails and places to picnic or sit down for a spell was a wonderful place to clear the mind. Sarah picked out a large oak tree near the water and sat down under its massive arms that extended out in all directions around her.

The tree's sturdy and solid structure gave her a feeling of security and strength as she looked out over the vast expanse of water in front of her. This was a refuge to her although she didn't understand the symbolism of it like that. So many other times she had been surrounded by arms of a different sort which gave her the same feeling. These were unseen, although, and harder for Sarah to discern at this point in her life. The refuge there at the park that she could see would serve as a basis for understanding the invisible forces about her, which would guide her for the rest of her life.

On Saturday afternoon, Sarah went driving out in the country on the other side of the campus and found a small church building set up on a hill. The church could seat around sixty people and had a white exterior with a simple steeple. Behind the church, there was a small mobile home that she assumed must be the parsonage. Sarah didn't want to bother anyone so she only pulled into the gravel parking lot of the church and slowly backed up to give her time to look around some. As she was driving back down the road, she felt impressed that this was the church that she needed to attend while at the university.

Sunday morning arrived and was a beautiful, sunny day.

Sarah had gotten a good night's sleep and was ready to get out of the apartment and meet the people at the church. When she pulled in the parking lot beside the church, she was happily greeted by an older couple. John and Marilyn Green introduced themselves and then took Sarah inside with such eagerness as if to show off a new gift that they had received. Sarah really enjoyed singing the choruses and the hymns. She also was inspired by the pastor's message to live the kind of life that would be an example to others while she was in school. The congregation had become accustomed to students coming to the church and knew that what they needed more than anything was acceptance, love, and support while they were away from home. Everyone was so happy to see a new face and many of them had to get a big hug before she left after the service to go back to her apartment.

Sarah sat down to a tuna sandwich and salad for lunch that day and then decided to take a walk that afternoon on the campus. The campus had a large wooded, park area where a lot of the students went to study, play a game, or have a picnic. Large oak trees were spaced over the entire area along the flower gardens and a lawn that was perfectly manicured. A few dogs were running around with some kids playing with Frisbees and Nurf Balls. The Nurf Balls didn't last too long with those dogs grabbing them and fighting over them.

Sarah saw a couple sitting together under a tree. She watched them as best she could, without appearing to be nosey, just to see how they acted with one another. Having a dating relationship with someone was something that she wasn't accustomed to at all. She was afraid of allowing someone to get to know her that well because she really thought that she would be rejected. Sarah felt so alone on the inside and knew that she wanted to have someone with whom she could share her most intimate thoughts. On the outside, however, she projected a sense of independence to give the impression that she didn't need anyone. She didn't understand, at the time, why she behaved that way. Sarah was frequently frustrated with herself because of this inability to have a truly meaningful relationship with someone.

She felt a little down after thinking about that and decided that she would walk over to the bookstore which was nearby on campus. Sarah already knew which classes that she would be starting the next day, so she decided that she would go ahead and get her books to start studying that afternoon. After she got back, she made her a hot glass of herbal tea and sat back in a comfortable chair to read for a while. She avoided having to address things that bothered her by getting her mind on a different topic. That behavior pattern enabled her to do well with her school work, but it surely took its toll on her personal life. God used that to help her stay focused on what He wanted her to learn for a greater purpose later in her life. She didn't know it then, but He would help her to change when it was needed.

After reading for a while, she decided that she would call Angie to see how she was doing where she was in school. They talked for about an hour and it was a great time for them both to catch up on what had been happening. Angie had become very active at the campus she was attending and even had a boyfriend, Scott, who she really liked a lot. Angie told Sarah all about Scott, how many clubs she belonged to, and how active she was in various areas. Angie had gotten a part-time job, too, at a local dress shop which she enjoyed and it gave her some extra spending money.

It seemed to Sarah that Angie was fitting in really good with the rest of her campus and making new friends easily. Sarah became frustrated with herself because she hadn't been able to feel included like Angie was able to do. Angie knew Sarah well enough to sense that she was feeling down because Sarah was only listening to her and not talking much. Angie quit talking so much about herself then, and tried to encourage Sarah to just go out and try to be friends with others so that she would have friends. It was a lot easier for Angie to do and she couldn't understand why it was so difficult for Sarah, but she was a good enough friend to try to understand. Angie knew that it would have been better for Sarah if she had gone to the same school, but Sarah had to learn how to make friends without regard for her location or circumstances. Whenever they would talk, Angie would always encourage Sarah to make some effort. Sarah knew that Angie was right and did get out and make more attempts to participate in some social activities.

Sarah went to the student union on some nights and weekends so that she could get out of the apartment and study in a different environment. She also went there so that she would have a chance to maybe meet some other people. Sarah felt so insecure with herself that she found it almost impossible to go up to someone else and initiate a conversation. She would sit at the table or in the lounge chair where she would study and just hope that someone would come and talk with her. After studying for a while, she would usually go back to her apartment having spoken to hardly anyone. It was so ironic that someone with such a need for a relationship would hold back from making any moves to achieve what she needed.

Even on Sundays, when she would go to church, some of the other folks there would introduce her to other people her age, but Sarah felt so awkward in trying to carry on a conversation with anyone new that she just met. Sarah really felt that she would be rejected by anyone that got to know her well, so she decided to not even try to start a close relationship. It was so much easier to have just an acquaintance with someone rather than to take a risk that someone would reject her again. Sarah had become accustomed to her own little world that she felt secure inside and it would literally take an act of God for that world she formed to be broken into pieces. Sarah couldn't truly be useful to Him until she had been completely remolded and that was something that only He could do the right way.

Sarah did very well in her studies and caught the attention of many of her instructors who could tell how dedicated she was to doing her best. She learned so much and was able to practically find applications for her knowledge that she acquired. So many of the other students would learn the material, but then could not apply that knowledge to life situations. The courses that she had during the third and fourth years were much more oriented to the subject of psychology and she enjoyed them much more.

One important skill that Sarah was accustomed to already was listening. She had a lot of experience in listening to others and not near as much in talking. That served her well in learning how to counsel with people. If she was only just as good at listening to herself and understanding herself, she would be able to help herself, and then others, too.

The time passed so rapidly that it seemed like just a few months and then she was graduating summa cum laude with a Bachelor of Arts degree in psychology. Sarah's grandparents and great-grandparents were all able to attend the graduation and were so proud of her accomplishments. They stayed the rest of the day with her and all of them went to eat at an Italian restaurant that evening. Sarah was happy to have this milestone behind her now and she enjoyed the time that she had with her relatives.

She had looked so forward to accomplishing this goal. It had finally happened, but the peace and happiness that she thought it would bring to her was fleeting. She went home that night pleased with herself, but a certain amount of emptiness still was there. Her relatives had left to drive the few hours back home and she was left there by herself. She thought that achieving something like this would help to fill a void that she wasn't sure how to fill, but it didn't.

Sarah had already decided that she would stay at the

university and pursue getting a master's degree and then a doctorate degree in psychology so that she could easily get a job as a counselor when she was finished. Finding a place to work without those additional degrees would be very difficult, she learned. Sarah sometimes would look at the amount of time it was taking to get through all of the courses and be tempted to get impatient and quit, but then she would remind herself to set a short-term goal that she could achieve first without thinking about the whole process and the entire amount of time it would take. She was excited because all of her course work now would be in the field that she enjoyed the most. She would able to have more exposure and access to the professors on the campus since she would now be a graduate student.

CHAPTER SEVENTEEN

Finding Someone to Love

Sarah was walking down one of the sidewalks on campus as soon as the new semester started when someone came running up from behind her and lightly pulled on the back of her hair. Sarah was startled and quickly turned around to see this dark-haired man who had a big smile on his face. He told her that he was so glad to see her again and Sarah had a look on her face of bewilderment. It took her a minute, but then she remembered back to when this boy in her hometown school would always sneak up behind her and pull her ponytail. She looked right into his eyes and then she instantly knew who he was. Those glowing, blue eyes were the same ones that used to glare at her from across the lunchroom. Sarah suddenly sprouted the biggest smile on her face and punched him on the arm like she used to do when she would catch him back then. It was Patrick.

Sarah couldn't believe that he was there at the same school as her. Patrick told her that he had transferred from another university and was going to the graduate school there now. Sarah was shocked even more when Patrick said that he was in the same program as her. She had always liked Patrick and it certainly brightened her day, no, her week, when she learned he would be there right at the same school. She remembered back at how he always picked on her when they were younger and how she grew to like the attention that he showed her. As they stood there gazing, smiling, and chatting to one another, Sarah felt as though a well was springing up within her of new life. She would have never thought that seeing Patrick would have made her feel this way. Maybe it was the thought of times past when life was simpler, or maybe it was just knowing that someone who knew her a little better than anyone else on the campus was now there close by. She had thought about him every once in a while, but so many years had passed since they were kids.

Patrick told Sarah how pretty that he thought she had become and she turned as red as a beet. She wasn't used to getting compliments like that at all. They talked for a few more minutes and then Patrick asked her if she would go out to eat with him sometime soon so that they could catch up on what had happened to each of them over the last several years. Sarah nervously wrote down and then gave him her telephone number and address. She was so excited on the inside that she was about to pop, but didn't want to show her true desperation to Patrick so she kept her emotions at bay. They parted ways that day with each of them having a sense of expectancy about what would develop with their relationship over the next several weeks and months ahead.

Sarah walked away with lightness in her walk as if she were walking on clouds. After she got back to her apartment she plopped down on her couch and laid there just thinking about memories of being a kid during the time that Patrick was in school with her. Seeing him again after such a long time brought back a lot of good memories of the times that they had at school. She was so excited about the thought of maybe having found someone that she could enjoy having a relationship with.

After she ate supper that night, Sarah leaped from where she was sitting when the phone rang because she was hoping it would be Patrick calling. It was him calling and they talked for about two hours that night. Before their conversation ended, Patrick and Sarah agreed to see each other on a date the next weekend. He told her that they could go to a little restaurant that he wanted to keep secret until then so he could surprise her. Sarah had to take a sleeping medication to even rest that night because she was so excited.

Sarah had been praying to find the right person with whom she could share her life. She already knew that the awards and degrees weren't going to bring any lasting joy and had been praying for what she needed to help bring her some peace into her life. Sarah knew when she was laying there in bed that He was answering a prayer for her. Before she went to sleep, she thanked Him for sending someone her way. Sarah had depended upon Him a lot already and now He was putting someone right in her path that she didn't realize then would be a refuge for her. She knew that God was her refuge, but He knew that she needed a helpmate, too.

The weekend came around after what seemed like a month to Sarah because she was really anticipating getting to spend time with Patrick. When he picked her up in his car that Saturday afternoon, Sarah told him that she wanted to take him to the park where she liked to go a lot. She wanted to show him that big tree under which she sat a lot of times when she needed to think or pray, or sometimes to study her books. After they had looked and walked around the park for about an hour, Sarah kept trying to figure out a way to get Patrick to tell her where he was going to be taking her that night. He wouldn't fall for any tricks, although, and just smiled at her saying she'd have to wait to find out.

Earlier in the week, Patrick had gotten in touch with Susan to try to find out about what Sarah liked so he could really surprise her without having to ask her himself. Susan was so excited that Sarah had met him, and she had told everyone else in the whole family about it. They all knew that Sarah was going out on a date soon, but couldn't say anything to her on the telephone if they talked. Sarah had talked to Elizabeth once during the week, but didn't tell her much other than she had a date that weekend. Elizabeth acted surprised and told her that she hoped she had a good time. Elizabeth enjoyed being in on a secret like this and snickered about it the whole week with the rest of the family.

While they were driving from the park, Sarah took note of all the turns that they were taking in her effort to try to figure it out. But Patrick had been clever and went a different route rather than a direct one. He had found out from Susan that Sarah had talked once about how she envisioned a romantic dinner would be. Patrick talked with one of his friends that he had met at college and had learned about this restaurant called Genny's about twenty-one miles from the campus.

The old, red brick building was nestled in the middle of some big oak trees and was situated right next to a creek that could be seen flowing out back. It was small and could seat only about thirty people. There was even a fireplace which warmed the room where the candlelit tables were arranged far enough apart so that diners could have some privacy. Patrick was pleased that Sarah was so happy with where they were. She told him that the surprise was well worth the wait and the anticipation. This was the ideal restaurant to her and she was so glad to be there with Patrick that she didn't care what they had for their meal. She just wanted to get to know him more.

They sat and talked for about two hours at the restaurant just picking at their food. It didn't seem like that much time had passed to them. After leaving the restaurant, Patrick took her back to the park that she loved going to so much. They walked down to that big oak tree close to the lake and Patrick sat down under the tree in the spot where Sarah normally liked to sit. Sarah sat in front of him and they leaned back on the tree as he held her in his arms. She could not have had a better feeling of love and security for that moment. As they sat, they talked about just about anything that came to their minds as they tried to learn what each other were really like. The time had gotten late before they knew it; it was one o'clock in the morning before they left the park. Patrick drove them to Sarah's apartment where he walked her to the door and really hated that he had to say good night. He kissed her once and she felt as though she would just melt into his arms if she could have. They reluctantly pulled themselves from one another and Patrick drove back to the campus dormitory where he lived.

Sarah had never met anyone that seemed to care so much for her. She had needed someone to truly love her for who she was for a long time. After they said goodbye for the night, she went inside and got ready for bed. She could hardly sleep as she thought about Patrick and whether this was just too good to be true. Sarah still didn't think enough of herself to believe that there was enough good about her for someone like Patrick to really love if he got to know her too well. She couldn't accept the reality of the respect that he had shown her and that he really seemed to care about her. She was a little suspicious that he had some other motivation that he hadn't revealed. The more that she stayed awake that night thinking about how meaningful the night was to her, she realized that this was a relationship that she certainly wanted to continue. She slept well after that time of thought and awoke the next morning feeling refreshed like she hadn't for a while.

Sarah found herself enjoying her classes even more than she had before and there seemed to be a new purpose to what she was doing. Routine tasks took on a new light and things that used to be upsetting didn't seem to be quite so bothersome. Her work seemed so different to her, too. Sarah knew that the way that she was feeling was something totally different than anything that she had felt before. It scared her, in a way, to feel so happy. She wondered if this would really last and she certainly hoped that the wonderful way that she was feeling would not only continue, but would get even better.

Sarah had lived long enough to know that this mountain that she seemed to be on top of now would certainly be surrounded by valleys all around. She just hoped that the top of this mountain would be wide and the travel across it would be slow, because the trip down the side wasn't what she wanted to do now. However, to get to that next mountain, that may be an even a greater height, necessitated that she travel down the side into the valley. A time in the valley was a time to look up in amazement and wonder at what was ahead to climb and not a time to look down dwelling on the depth that she would be then. Keeping her vision focused on the light above would guide her through the valleys that lay ahead. She would get stronger all along the journey ahead by having a committed plan of never being content to stop anywhere along the trip of life, but to always forge ahead in spite of whatever circumstances came her way. The light above that she used to guide her way was dim sometimes, but as she would travel it would become brighter and the path would be clearer.

Patrick and Sarah spent time together most weekends and some weeknights. Since they were both in the same program at the university, they were able to help each other with studying for tests and preparing different assignments. Sarah took Patrick to the church where she had been attending and he really enjoyed worshipping there with the other members. The time seemed to go faster and faster for them both. Sarah remembered back to when she heard her grandmother say that as she got older the time went faster; she didn't believe it then, but she was now starting to understand.

She and Patrick had been there for a year already, but when she was thinking about it, it seemed like she had known him for so much longer. It was hard for her to think of a time when he wasn't there, or to imagine living life now without him. She knew that she had fallen in love.

Patrick treated her with such respect. Sarah had shared with him bits and pieces of her troubled past, but hadn't told him everything yet. Patrick could tell that it was a hurtful subject for her to discuss, so he was very patient in allowing her to reveal more about herself as she felt like it. Since he was at the same school when she was younger, he had heard different things about her from his friends talking, but he knew that there was more to the story than the usual gossip in which so many people engage.

They shared some tender moments together when Patrick could tell that Sarah was having a time of feeling down. He would hold her sometimes as she would just cry. Little by little he learned more about Sarah and why she had become who she was. Sometimes she would seem irritable to him, but he learned that that was when she was really bothered by something that was on her mind, or when the past was haunting her. He would gently inquire about what was of such concern to her; after a few minutes, she would start talking and would feel better knowing that he cared enough to listen.

Patrick had always been more expressive about how he felt and still was. Sarah needed someone like him to help her become more open with her feelings. Patrick had similar thoughts of how he was a better person since meeting Sarah, too. He was less serious about everything than her. He felt that he was improved by having a relationship with her because she helped him to become a better steward of his time and resources.

They talked about their dreams and their goals in life. Sarah had become so high-minded about what she wanted to do with her life. Patrick had told her that he was content to get out of school and have a good paying job along with a loving family. There was certainly nothing wrong with that, but to Sarah it just wasn't good enough. She was intent on not living the life that everyone else lives. She didn't just want to get by; she wanted to excel in whatever she did. She had spent so much time in her studies and in disciplining herself before she met Patrick. Trying to change her habits now would be difficult.

All that Sarah had before which she could trust and feel secure in was her work. Now she had Patrick to trust in and he sure did make her feel secure. She kept thinking about the time that he went with her to the park and sat under that big oak tree. It was the same oak tree that had become a refuge to her when she was troubled. Sarah trusted God to help her in everything, but having a physical presence like that tree seemed to reinforce it to her. When Patrick sat under that tree and then held out his arms for her so he could hold her, it was as if to her that he was unknowingly becoming a substitute for that strong oak tree. Yes, He was answering her prayer and she was finding the person that would be a refuge for her.

She had poured out her heart so many times under that tree, and it could not talk back. God had heard every word and seen every tear, although. She wondered sometimes if He did hear her. She wondered why He didn't seem near occasionally, or why answers to her prayers seemed so long in coming. Now she had someone that could listen to her and comfort her. She thanked Him for sending Patrick her way.

After they had been seeing each other for over a year, Patrick invited Sarah to go with him to his parents' house for Christmas that year. She certainly accepted and they traveled down together. His parents still lived in the same house where he had grown up and it was only a few miles from Sarah's folks. Everyone in each of their families was buzzing with excitement over this new romance. Elizabeth scurried around wanting to hear from Sarah, or from any other family member who talked to Sarah, every tidbit of information that she could get. It made her remember when she was young and falling in love to hear about it all. Patrick's parents, Tommy and Carol, were so excited to finally get to meet Sarah. He had been telling them a lot about her and she was everything to them that he had said. They all had a great time getting to know one another during that holiday break. Even Sarah's folks came over to Patrick's for Christmas dinner that year. It seemed to Sarah like she had found some wholeness in her life and it came to her when she felt she had needed it the most.

After the Christmas break was over and they were back at the university again, each of them knew that their relationship was certainly changed forever. They knew that there was what could be described as a deepening effect about going to be with each other's family. It allowed for both of them to know that there was a true seriousness about what one thought about the other. It made them have considerations of progression to a greater level between them. How the rest of the family felt about the relationship could make it work, or fail. Fortunately, each side of the family was compatible with the other, and they really enjoyed the short time of being together for that Christmas season. Sarah and Patrick both knew that their relationship was maturing to the point of some very serious decisions having to be made soon.

Patrick had dated a few other girls before, but he had never met anyone with whom he had so much respect. Sarah was a beautiful girl, but she didn't act like she knew it; he liked that about her. Patrick thought about how she knew her studies so well and was so dedicated to doing her best in her work. He admired her integrity, concern for others, and genuine faith which guided her life. Sarah certainly wasn't perfect, but she seemed almost so to Patrick. The more time that Patrick spent thinking about Sarah and spending time with her, he realized that he was falling more and more in love with her as the days went by. He found himself thinking constantly about her when he was away from her.

What he could do next to make her happy was a frequent thought when he should have been studying more. After a while, Patrick began to think about proposing marriage. His parents had already told him about what a catch Sarah would be and that he better not let her get away from him. He knew that the analogy of fishing was somewhat appropriate for he had been out at a pond before and had made the mistake of having a good fish hooked only to be lost while he was playing around instead of working on reeling it in.

Sarah definitely knew that she loved Patrick. He had been everything that she had needed for so many times in her life. The weekend after they came back from the Christmas holiday, she was relaxing in her bed Saturday morning. Just laying there and not wanting to get up yet, she thought about all the great moments that they had together.

She remembered back a couple of months before, when Patrick had shown up at her door one Saturday morning. He knew that she wasn't feeling well and was determined that he was going to help lift her spirits since she was feeling down. Sarah had answered the door and was embarrassed that she wasn't ready to greet anyone in public yet, but it didn't seem to matter to Patrick. She felt like he accepted her for who she really was; he knew her weak points and seemed to care for her anyway. After he finally convinced her to let him inside, it wasn't long before he had fixed up a wonderful breakfast for them both. He even helped clean up the kitchen before he left to get some work done for the rest of the day. Also, he didn't leave before he talked her into going out with him that night, too.

Sarah liked his persistence and patience with her. She

had not been the most loveable person in the beginning, but he seemed to see through all of that. Patrick understood her heart and Sarah knew that he loved her. There wasn't a better feeling to her than to know that fact. Sarah spent about an hour that Saturday morning thinking about their relationship. She, too, knew that some serious decisions had to be made in the near future. Little did she know how quickly things were starting to go for them both.

After Patrick had talked more with his parents and a close friend in his dormitory, he prayed for wisdom in making the right decision. He felt at ease by that Sunday morning when he picked up Sarah for them to go to church together. Sarah had wondered what was on Patrick's mind that entire week after they had gotten back because she could tell that he was preoccupied in his thoughts about something. Sarah was afraid sometimes that he had seen too much during the Christmas break with her family and was starting to have second thoughts about her. She was glad to see him that Sunday morning when he arrived, and noticed that he seemed much happier than usual. She didn't know that he had resolved a critical decision in his mind during that week.

They had a great time at the worship service that day and spent the afternoon at the park. Sarah kept wondering why Patrick was different that day. He seemed so much more at peace to her about something, but she couldn't tell about what. When she would ask, he told her that he just felt good that day and was glad he could be with the girl that he loved. Sarah smiled as big as she possibly could when he said that. The peace that he felt within himself was wearing off onto her, too.

The week ahead of them was busy and they didn't see each other much during the week because of some projects that were due. By the time that the weekend had come, Sarah was wondering what they would do together then. She always found herself with those new thoughts, instead of before when she would only think about what the next week's work would be. Patrick hadn't told her much about what he had thought about doing that weekend. Usually he told her ahead of time about what he was thinking of doing, and was seeing what she wanted to do. Sarah was a little nervous because she knew that he was up to something.

Patrick had been doing a lot of thinking during that week trying to plan the perfect way to propose to Sarah. There was a beautiful mountainous area a few hours from the university. Right after lunch that Saturday, Patrick picked up Sarah and they drove for about two and a half hours until they got to these curving, narrow roads that led further and further up into the mountains. He had learned from a friend about a secluded area where there was a waterfall that was accessible by a narrow, dirt pathway through lush undergrowth. Sarah hadn't been to that area before and was excited to be up in the mountains. She could tell that this was a special trip for them by the way that Patrick was acting about it, but she certainly wasn't expecting what was ahead.

When they arrived at the site where the waterfall was said to be located, Patrick and Sarah looked around at what seemed upon initial inspection like just any other road side. Patrick hoped that his information hadn't been wrong. He surveyed around and then saw the old metal gate that he was told was the entrance. The old gate wouldn't open so they had to climb over it and then walked down this pathway through a field. It wasn't long before they came upon an area where there was a thick wooded region with the pathway meandering right up into it. There was such a stark contrast between these two areas of the pathway—a totally new journey was just up ahead.

The pathway was surrounded by such beautiful vegetation and flowers that gave off a perfume like they hadn't smelled before. After about three hundred feet from entering the wooded area, they noticed that the air had an increase in humidity with a visible mist all about them. They could hear the roar of rushing water and then saw through all the leaves and branches the foamy, white water down the hill that they were climbing. When they got to the top of the hill, they were able to see such a spectacular view of the waterfall. They could hardly believe that a place as nice as this had no other visitors there to enjoy it.

When they got up to the top of the hill, they were able to walk to the edge of the waterfall and climb out on some flat rocks where the water was shallow. It was about 60 degrees outside, but Patrick had to go wading in the water anyway in spite of Sarah's advice that it was too cold. He knew he wouldn't be back at that site for a long time and wanted to enjoy it as much as he could. Patrick also was pretty hyped up about the evening ahead and had enough adrenaline flowing that it didn't feel cold at all to him. In fact, he probably needed a little cooling down. Sarah stayed as dry as she could and found an elevated rock further down toward the edge of the waterfall that was a great place to sit.

Patrick saw her sitting on the rock and could tell that she was in deep thought about something as she looked out over the water cascading down to the stream below. He went down where she was and sat on the rock with her. As he held her hand, he told her how much he loved her. Sarah had such a sad look on her face all of the sudden. Patrick certainly hoped that telling her that he loved her would bring a better reaction than that. He asked her what was wrong that would make her sad when they were surrounded by such beauty. Patrick had learned that Sarah's sense of self worth wasn't what it should be. She finally told him that she didn't feel like she deserved someone who was so good to her like Patrick was. She was sad because so many of the good things in her life hadn't lasted. Sarah was actually enjoying herself and she did love Patrick. Somehow though, she felt like she shouldn't be enjoying herself, or having fun like she was. She looked out over the water that rushed so fast down the waterfall and thought about how time seemed to rush by just as fast. Life that was there in front of her at one second was gone in the next. She actually felt a sense of guilt about it and thought about her dad, mom, and brother who had all died so tragically. Sarah obviously was still having trouble with letting go of the past and being able to enjoy the present.

Patrick could sense this struggle within Sarah. He knew that the best thing for her was for him to show her that he really did love her. He wanted to show her that he loved her not through words alone, but through actions. He gave her a big hug as a few tears welled up in both of their eyes. They both knew that they had something special and something that so many never find. Sitting there holding each other for a few minutes said more than words could have expressed as Patrick tried to convey to Sarah that he was not leaving and that he was committed to her.

When they were leaving the waterfall area, they skipped down the path holding hands. Both of them were so happy that they had found one another. When they were getting close to the car, this gigantic German Shepherd dog started barking from out of the woods and then came running at them. Patrick didn't know that Sarah could run so fast; she beat him back to the car. The doors were locked and Patrick had the keys so he ran to the passenger side first to let Sarah inside. Patrick was going to try to run back around to the driver side, but the dog was getting too close for him to be able to make it. He had to pile into the car on Sarah's side and barely got the door shut before the dog was there. Patrick had basically pushed Sarah over and was just about on top of her as he had made a mad dash to get away from that big dog.

They were both laughing about the close call and then Sarah reached over and gave Patrick a big kiss that he wasn't expecting. She had recognized that he had come out of his way to let her in the car first. That told her that he did care about her and was going to protect her; she knew then that his words did mean something. She knew to an even greater degree that he did love her. Sarah thought about how her name would sound if it was different. *Sarah Ashton does sound pretty good.*

After they both calmed down from the excitement, Patrick drove them down the mountain side to a restaurant located right beside a stream. The stream had trout in it and persons coming there could even catch their own fish if they desired. Sarah told Patrick that she had rather not have to catch and then see what she was going to eat so they opted to just have the meal prepared without going fishing. They did go and sit next to the stream there, although, while waiting for supper to be served. Patrick had ordered plates that they could take with them. After they got the plates, they drove back up the curvy roads along the mountain side in the same direction as the waterfall. Sarah asked Patrick where they were going now and he told her that she would still have to wait and see.

It was getting dark already, but he was able to see well enough to find this apple orchard along side the road. Patrick had planned the whole day and this was to be the spot where he was going to ask the big question. He had brought a blanket and some candles with them. After getting parked and then finding a spot for their picnic, Patrick lit the candles and they said a blessing for their meal as they sat right across from each other. They had grilled trout, green beans, mashed potatoes, and toast. The food was good, but neither of them was much interested in eating. They mostly just picked at the food because Patrick was nervous about what he was about to ask. Sarah could tell something was on his mind and so her mind was preoccupied wondering why he was so fidgety.

The candles brought a little bit of warmth to them as they cuddled up together next to them. As they sat there a while, they were starting to feel the chilliness of the 55 degree weather outside. Patrick had brought his Bible with him that night and had decided that he wanted to share some scripture with Sarah as part of his proposal. He read from Psalm 55: "*Give ear to my prayer, O God, and do not hide Yourself from my supplication. Attend to me, and hear me; I am restless in my complaint, and moan noisily, because of the voice of the enemy, because of the oppression of the wicked; for they bring down trouble upon me, and in wrath they hate me. My heart is severely pained within me, and the terrors of death have fallen upon me. Fearfulness and trembling have come upon me, and horror has overwhelmed me. So I said, "Oh, that I had wings like a dove! I would fly away and be at rest. Indeed, I would wander far off, and remain in the wilderness. I would hasten my escape from the windy storm and tempest" (Psalm 55:1-8 NKJV).*

As Patrick read the scripture, Sarah could see by the little bit of light that they had from the candles and hear from the way he spoke that he had thought a lot about those verses. She could sense a kindred spirit within him as he felt tossed about sometimes, just like her, by the storms of life raging all about them. They both knew that they had an enemy around them who "*walks about like a roaring lion, seeking whom he may devour" (I Peter 5:8/ NKJV)*. Patrick told her then how he knew she had struggled with those feelings herself, just like he had. He explained to her how his faith had helped him so much in his life and how he had prayed before coming to the university that he would be led to the person in his life that God wanted him to be with for the rest of his life.

Sarah almost melted as she realized that he felt the same way that she did. She had been praying to find that person whom He had for her. Patrick told her that, just like in the scripture, they both wanted to fly away sometimes and be at rest. He told her that the life we live here is wrought with troubles, but they could weather the storms together under the Rock that is a shelter and shield for all who ask for it. Patrick helped her see that unlike the lone dove that wants to fly away, two doves together could successfully make it with His help.

As Patrick held her close, he told her that he wanted to be that dove there with her. He wanted to be someone that she could depend upon, could trust in fully, and could be a refuge for her. Sarah was almost in tears from the joy that she felt inside. She knew then that Patrick truly understood her and had no doubt that he did love her for who she was. As they looked into one another's eyes, Patrick opened up a little black box with a diamond ring inside that gleamed in the candle light. He asked her if she would commit to spending the rest of her life with him in a marriage that he felt God had arranged.

Sarah had suspicions that he might be going to propose soon, but really thought they were just going out on a date that weekend. She was a little stunned when those words came out and she actually heard him ask for her hand in marriage. She still believed that having him in her life was something that was too good to be true and, somehow, subconsciously had felt that it wouldn't last. Now she was hearing with her own ears what she really had hoped in the depths of her heart would be true. It took her a minute or two to absorb the significance of the moment. It was like she had instant replay going over all of their time together, especially that weekend. Patrick was wondering if she was going to answer and he held her close to him as he silently prayed that she would know the right answer.

Sarah pulled back from Patrick just enough to look directly into his eyes as she told him through her tears, and a glowing smile, that she was accepting him as her life mate for all of their lives while on earth. They spent some time just holding one another as they looked up into the heavens above and were in awe that He would even take the time to care so much about them. Sarah's refuge in Him was complimented now by the refuge that Patrick was to her, too. Life had never felt better for them both.

CHAPTER EIGHTEEN

Patrick & Sarah Together

Patrick and Sarah decided that they wanted to get married in May of the next year close to the date of when Julia and Frank, Sarah's parents, were married. That gave them seven months to prepare for the wedding. Patrick thought it was plenty of time, but Sarah kept telling him how hard it was going to be to get everything together. All of the relatives of each of them were so excited about this new development and it gave them all something to talk about everywhere they went. Sarah's folks were the most excited because they had worried and prayed for so long that Sarah would find peace. They could tell that she was troubled and anything that would help her like this was something that was nothing more to them than an answer to prayer.

It only took until the next weekend before Susan and Elizabeth had driven to the apartment at the university where Sarah lived. They had to all get together and decide on the plans for the wedding ceremony. Susan cherished every moment of getting to share on planning for something so important to Sarah. Being able to help with this was something that Susan didn't get to do with Julia. She had so many regrets of the time that she didn't spend with Julia and the hurt feelings between them that never had been mended. This was a small, but significant, way for Susan to be able to make up for her inattention in the past. It helped Susan more than Sarah realized to be able to be a part of her life.

Patrick had it the easiest since he was the groom. As tradition had it, he had to only worry about the rehearsal dinner, having the tuxedo ready for the big day, and then the honeymoon plans. Seeing all the frantic activity of the ladies made him wonder why it had to be such an ordeal. He secretly wished they could just go and get married, and not have to go through with all of the ceremony. However, Patrick knew that it meant so much to so many others, so he didn't say anything, except to Sarah, and she quickly dismissed the notion.

Sarah planned for the wedding to be held in a little, white, wood-frame Nazarene chapel up near the mountains where they had gotten engaged. They decided that there was no one better to perform the ceremony than Pastor Mickey Davis. He was Sarah's pastor from when she was born and through some tumultuous times. Bro. Mickey had moved from that church to another state which was close enough by that Patrick and Sarah had visited with him one weekend a few months back. Patrick had never met him before, but did remember how he had helped a next-door neighbor when he was pastoring there several years back. He helped so many people that didn't even come to the church where he pastored and had garnered a great deal of respect in the area that he shepherded. Sarah never had realized before all the details that had to go into getting all of the plans together for everything needed. Trying to juggle her work at the university with getting arrangements made was difficult. It would have been harder for her if it hadn't been for Susan helping so much. Elizabeth helped as much as she could, but it was harder for her to get around like she did before.

They all had such a great time planning the wedding.

It seemed like hardly any time had passed at all before the wedding day had arrived. Before the ceremony, Patrick was getting tired of all of the pictures that he had to endure having taken, but finally made it through them. When the big moment of walking out of that back room and in front of the congregation with Pastor Davis came, he was pretty nervous. He was in awe at the significance of what was about to take place. It was an historic event that he knew would forever alter his life and the life of Sarah.

He knew that it was to be until physical death and that what God had placed together, no man should put asunder. He knew that it would have to be the death of living for himself, and the same for Sarah, with a new life of oneness together if their marriage would last and be the example of Christ and His Church that God intended for marriage to represent. He knew that he was supposed to be the spiritual leader and might have the responsibility of raising children one day. He knew how much Sarah needed him to be strong for her. A moment of such significance certainly had given Patrick much to think about.

His best man, a good friend named Winston, stood there to the side of him as the pastor was about to speak. Sarah came down the center aisle dressed as beautiful as he had ever seen her. All of those thoughts were flooding through his mind so fast that he could hardly process them all. She was up there and standing next to him before he could take it all in. He wished that the whole thing could be put into slow motion so that he could savor each moment.

As Pastor Davis spoke to them about what marriage really meant, they both looked into each other's eyes and could each tell that they shared the same thoughts without having to even speak to each other. When the vows of commitment to each other and to God were read, they each answered "I will," except that Patrick had to add some extra meaning to his commitment and replied with "I will - forever." After the rings were exchanged, they held each other's hands as a special song was sung by a friend.

Patrick was overwhelmed with so many emotions of it all that he couldn't help but to cry. It was such a wonderful thing that had just happened that he could only cry when he thought about how undeserving he was of who the Lord had provided for him to marry. He was humbled at Sarah's love for him and even more humbled at God's love for him. If one thought about it with that kind of significance, one could only cry, not out of sadness, but out of an extreme of joy, wonder, and awe.

It hardly seemed like any time before they were walking down the aisle and Patrick noticed that quite a few others had shared his feelings. He could tell that they, too, knew how he felt. Some were older and had been married for decades while others for lesser periods, but many of them told him during the reception that they were glad he was taking seriously what was done that day. They both thought about how so many couples didn't seem to remember their commitment to each other, and to God, that they made with good intentions when they started out. When the pressures of life came, unless the house had been built upon the right foundation to start with, it would not be able to stand up to the storms that would inevitably come.

Patrick and Sarah both knew that God had placed them together. One of their wedding gifts was a painting from a friend of two doves perched together under a rock next to the ocean which was being tossed about by a dark storm. Lightening flashed across the sky and high waves nipped at the edges of the shelter under the rock where they cuddled together. It was a scene that surely would have been the end of them both if it hadn't been for that cover in the cleft of the rock. A lighthouse in the distance was visible through all of the darkness of the storm raging about them. Sometimes it was barely visible and sometimes it was so bright that it was visible from anywhere, but as long as they knew where to look and kept their eyes on that lighthouse, it was never hidden from them. Many other gifts were given to them at the reception, but that was probably the one with the most meaning to them both. That painting would remind them in the years ahead of where they needed to look, and sometimes where they needed to hide, together.

When the reception was nearing an end, they proceeded out for the traditional send-off. Patrick had hidden Sarah's car that they were using to travel to their honeymoon spot. He was glad that he did after seeing his truck covered with all of the shaving cream and cans that he could stand. Someone had even put an open can of sardines under the hood that they found after desperately trying to find out from where that awful smell was coming. Patrick knew that his prankster friend, Brian, had struck again. Patrick and Sarah took the truck to a friend's house and changed their clothes before getting into the car and leaving together as husband and wife.

Patrick had thought for quite a while about where they could go for their honeymoon. He wanted to go somewhere quiet, peaceful, and it certainly had to be romantic. After talking with Pastor Davis in the prior weeks, he learned about a cabin further up in the mountains and right up the road from where he had proposed to Sarah. The cabin was built right over the side of a rapidly flowing stream that could be heard from the inside. The stream also happened to be not too far of a walk downstream from the very waterfall that Patrick and Sarah had visited together. Inside the cabin, there was a small kitchen near the front, a small dining area to the right, and a living area in the back with windows all along the back wall overlooking the stream. A wood-burning stove kept the place as warm as they wanted and to the side of the living area was the single bedroom and bathroom of the cabin.

Getting away from the life of the university campus for a week was good by itself, but being able to spend the whole week with a new spouse was something that felt just too good to be true. Patrick kept thinking about how they both had a whole week up there away from everything. They hadn't really planned much in the way of activities during the week because they wanted to spend time with each other and just go and do whatever they felt like each day. Being able to sleep late and not have to get up and go do anything was a good feeling.

They were glad that they hadn't committed all of their time together to so many activities that they didn't have time to spend with one another just being with each other. Watching each other as they splashed around in the stream nearby and feeling the guidance of a hand to keep each other steady when there was uneven footing were moments that couldn't be scheduled or bought. They delighted in sitting outside and watching the glory of a beautiful sunset while discussing how it's so reflective of His glory. Walking down the paths in the woods nearby the cabin allowed them to see His creation and realize that they were a part of it. They wondered in awe at how they had found each other and knew that the very God that had created what they beheld also took the time to love them and guide them. As they held each other close, each thanked Him for making it possible.

Patrick realized that he had a responsibility to be the spiritual leader of their new household. That thought didn't make him afraid, however, because he knew that he could not achieve what he needed to in his marriage through his own strength. It must be done with the strength and power provided by the Holy Spirit in his life. Patrick had learned a few years back that when he tried to handle matters in his own hands and with his own ideas, he usually made a mess of things. Learning to have enough patience to allow Him to do what He wanted to do in his own life and the lives of others was, to say the least, extremely helpful.

Sarah was so happy that she could hardly contain herself. She never thought she would have someone like Patrick and it was like she was living a dream now. Sometimes, she wondered if she was going to awaken and find out it wasn't true. Patrick had never been pushy with her. He had been patient all along to give her the time to learn to trust him and to learn to love him. When they were together during that honeymoon week, Patrick was careful to show Sarah the respect that he knew she needed to see in him. He knew about what had happened to her when Chris was her step-father and he realized that he needed to be everything to her that Chris never was, and never should have tried to have been. Sarah was nervous about their honeymoon together because of her past, but she quickly had those fears put to rest. She saw how much Patrick had the kind of love for her that she thought she'd only find when reading those Christian romance novels that she loved.

The week started and ended before they could hardly realize it, although. Patrick and Sarah both wished they had been able to take more time off because it passed so fast. They talked about how nice it would be to be able to spend the rest of their lives with each other alone on some deserted part of the planet. It would be different getting back into their studies now because they would be together and that fact certainly lessened the brunt of reality ahead of them again. They had gotten off to a good start together, but the road ahead would get rough. It was good that God decided to only show them just enough of the portion of the road ahead that they needed right at that time. Complete knowledge of what lay ahead was something only He could handle knowing.

They didn't have too much more to pack than when they arrived. Sarah had found a few trinkets that she liked when they had driven into a nearby town one day. Before they left, they set the camera on auto and took a picture sitting with one another in a chair in the living room of the cabin. They took some more pictures outside and then some more looking back down the road as they were leaving. Sarah had taken so many pictures during their stay that Patrick thought he'd never get them all developed. He would be glad later that she had taken them when the years had passed and then he could more easily remember the time of when they got started. It was a good start and a moment that they could think back about later when they needed a sense of direction.

When they arrived back on campus, it felt so odd to them that they were able to unpack and then stay together without one of them having to go home. Sharing the one apartment now would certainly be easier financially. Only about an hour after they had gotten back, Barbara and Jerry from the church in town they attended came by to welcome them home. They didn't come empty handed, either. Barbara had baked a fresh, steaming-hot, raspberry pie. They talked for a few minutes over a piece of pie and some coffee before getting back to work fixing up the place like they wanted it together.

They had two days left of their time off they had taken so that they could get settled on the new living arrangements. Those two days flew by, but they savored every moment knowing that they would never have to be apart again. They were up on the mountain then and didn't see the valley that was just ahead. God was being good to them because if He had shown them the troubles to come, the present moments couldn't have been enjoyed so much.

CHAPTER NINETEEN

Trial by Fire

Patrick and Sarah were married for about a year when they made a decision to try to have children. They talked together about all of their plans for how they would want to raise children and what they would want for them. They were just like any would-be parents who would want the best that could be for their children. At night before they would go to sleep, Sarah told Patrick how she wanted to have a chance to be a mother and provide things that she didn't have. She talked about the values that she wanted to teach them and the God that she wanted them to know. Patrick and Sarah both prayed for His will in the matter and committed it to Him. Even though they committed this to Him, they still expected that the usual turn of events would occur with them also. Just like their friends and most everyone else, they expected that within a few months they would find out that Sarah was going to have a child.

Their time at the university was nearing an end within a little over a year. They both had been trying to decide where they would go when their education there was finished. Since they both were completing degrees in psychology, they decided that they would open an office to provide counseling for people of all ages. Sarah had focused on child psychology while Patrick dealt with adults more in his training. Besides spending time talking about the children that they hoped to have, they discussed and dreamed about every facet of their life ahead after graduation.

One weekend after they had been reviewing newspapers and real estate guides, they took a trip down to the town where they had grown up. Both of them had decided that they wanted to be back home and around their family and the people who they knew the best. Patrick had found out about a piece of land for sale that they went to see. After looking at several areas, they found some land that was just perfect for them. It wasn't priced too badly and was located in an area with a good school district. They talked with the real estate agent and the seller agreed to their offer. Besides that, they talked with a contractor about getting a house built on the land by the time that would be moving down from the university. Excitement wasn't even the most descriptive word to emphasize how they both felt. This land would be where so many things would occur; their children would grow up and they would grow old together there. It all seemed so perfect.

After the legal and financial matters were settled with the land, they came down one weekend and stayed out on the land in a tent. They sat out by the fire, roasted marshmallows, and drank hot cider as they talked more about plans for their house and the bright future ahead of them. As the night got later, they held each other close under a blanket by the fire. They couldn't have been happier.

During that night together, Sarah knew in her inner-most being was a night when she conceived a child. Over the next several weeks, Sarah knew that her dream of having a child was a possibility. She was late having her cycle and a home pregnancy test confirmed her suspicions. They were both so happy that this part of their life also seemed to be working out like they had hoped. Their plans appeared to be working out for them, or so they seemed. They thought that the greenest pastures were ahead of them, but never suspected the desert up ahead.

They both attended a psychology conference when Sarah was about six weeks along in the pregnancy. The trip went well for them and they were enjoying learning new ideas during the various seminars they attended. The conference was held in Chicago which was a place that they had never been. During the afternoons, they went walking down the streets overshadowed by more tall buildings than they had ever seen in their lives. They walked so much that they had blisters on their feet.

Sarah started having some abdominal pain during the day before they were leaving. On the morning of their departure, she had some heavy bleeding and knew enough to know that she had had a miscarriage. They were both upset and were glad that they were heading back home. When they arrived back at the university, Sarah saw an obstetrician who confirmed what she had dreaded was the truth. When the doctor told Sarah that she had lost an early pregnancy, Patrick was there to hold her as the descent from the mountain top began. This was just the beginning of their trial together.

Sarah had always wanted to have children. When she was little she longed for the day when she would be "mommy" and carried around dolls all over the house. Julia would sprout a big smile when she would enter Sarah's room and find Sarah holding her favorite doll in the rocking chair. That caused Julia to remember back to when she used to hold Sarah in that same chair. Sarah had been able to keep that same rocking chair and had put it in a small room that she and Patrick had already renovated for the first newborn.

When they got home from the doctor, Sarah went to the

room where they already had their hearts set on seeing a little Sarah or Patrick stay. Sarah had been so happy during the early days of their marriage, but she longed for children. She wanted to raise them in a good family with a father that cared about them. That was something that she didn't have for very long early in her own life. Sarah walked around to the baby bed that they had already placed in the room and felt the emptiness in the bed. She then couldn't help but to feel like a part of her was missing. That rocking chair was close by the bed and Sarah slumped into it holding her face in her empty hands.

Patrick tried his best to console her. He even went and got her a little Scottish terrier puppy to keep her company; Sarah named her "Maggie." With all of their psychological training and knowledge, it still didn't make them immune to feeling the same hurts as everyone else and trying to understand their own emotions. Patrick knew that Sarah needed to grieve over this loss and he tried to give her the time that she required. With the passing days and weeks, he realized that her grief wasn't resolving in a healthy manner. She was hardly keeping up with her educational requirements and was slowly shutting out everyone, including Patrick. For some reason, Sarah had fallen into a depth of despair that they could only see worsening.

Instead of seeing the possibilities ahead, she saw the present loss. Instead of praising Him even during this time of not understanding, she questioned Him. Instead of drawing closer to Patrick for them both to become stronger, she became more reclusive. Those refuges that had provided security and protection in the past didn't help now because she didn't seek them. The joy that had been there was replaced by a sadness that seemed to have no end.

Patrick had wanted to call Susan and discuss Sarah's problem, so he was delighted when the phone rang on a weekday night when Sarah hadn't gotten home yet.

However, it wasn't the kind of call that would provide for some good advice on how to help Sarah. Susan told Patrick the bad news that Elizabeth had passed away in her sleep late that afternoon. Patrick had gotten to know Elizabeth well enough to know why she meant so much to Sarah. He didn't know how he would be able to tell her about this when she was already so depressed.

When Sarah arrived home, Patrick tried to be as bright as possible. They were in their new home, but it seemed so far from home. Sarah had made a sandwich and then had reclined to the couch. She was just picking at her food and timidly asked Patrick what was on his mind. She could tell that he had to tell her something, but she was fearful of what it was. Patrick slowly walked over, squatted down in front of her, and told her the bad news as he held her hands in his.

As Patrick had feared, the little bit of peace that Sarah was desperately trying to hold onto, disappeared. She withdrew her hands from his and buried her head under the cushions of the couch. Patrick leaned over and tried to hold her, but she didn't want anyone near her. Sarah told Patrick to leave her alone as she attempted to hold herself together enough to talk to him. Patrick left her to grieve as she requested, but not before reminding her, "I love you, Sarah, and we can get through this together if you'll let God help us. I know you don't understand and I don't either, but we have to trust God until it becomes clear."

The next few days were difficult to say the least. All of the memories that Sarah had tried to repress were coming back to her as she thought of the events of recent days. Elizabeth's death and the funeral brought back all of thoughts of Frank, Julia and Frank, Jr.'s deaths so many years ago. Having the loss of the pregnancy made her think about the loss of her own childhood. She couldn't help but to be reminded of the abuse that she endured from Chris.

She had a husband that loved her, but she felt more

alone now than ever. Susan talked with her and tried to help. Sarah hadn't been that close to her for so many years before and Elizabeth had been there for her when Susan hadn't been. One of Sarah's refuges wasn't there anymore. If she could have only remembered that He had provided for her through other sources of strength and encouragement. She felt like she was in pieces and needed someone to help put her back together again. Sarah was a Christian, but she didn't fully understand yet that He was the only One who knew how to put all of the pieces back together where they should go. Her real refuge and source of complete healing hadn't been found by her yet.

After the funeral, they came back home and things seemed to improve somewhat. They both got back into the routines of daily life, but Sarah poured herself more into her educational work to the neglect of Patrick. Patrick tried to be as patient with her as he could, but he could tell that she was choosing to handle the problems by ignoring them. Sarah didn't realize that all of the work that she did was a way of being distracted enough that she didn't have time to sit back and think about the torments within her mind that never left. Her soul yearned for healing and she wandered from one activity to the next in the hopes of finding fulfillment and a sense of purpose.

Patrick realized that Sarah had been repressing all of the things that bothered so much. She wasn't the same person that he had married and she was changing into someone that he wasn't sure of anymore. When she came home, she was distant from him emotionally and went through the activities of each day more as though they were chores, than being happy at being able to even perform them. She wasn't happy and Patrick couldn't help wondering if he was the cause of some of her discontentment. This time of trial was pulling them apart instead of bringing them together as it should have.

The stress of moving was upon them, too. Sarah didn't feel like having to make all of the decisions required by her with their house construction and begrudgingly muddled through it all as she sat back and wondered was it all worth it. The house was coming together beautifully and Patrick drove down on most weekends to get some things done, but Sarah usually stayed home. As Sarah pushed him away more, he stayed busy apart from her as he tried to understand what was happening to them both.

Patrick didn't know what else to do other than to pray for the Lord's intervention. Sarah tried to pray, but couldn't feel peace. Just as there is a top of the mountain, there is a bottom of the valley. With every place in that valley where Sarah tried to run, she couldn't see Him, but He was there. No matter where she would try to run, she wouldn't be able to escape Him. When she left this valley that seemed like ten thousand miles wide, she would not be the same ever again.

Graduation finally came and what should have been a celebration for them both was not filled with the joy that they would have thought earlier it would have been. Instead of being happy about achieving a goal, the thoughts then turned to what the next goal was. The journey that they were taking was fraught with the concerns and worries of making it to the next goal, or destination, instead of enjoying each day of the trip.

They moved down to their new house and leased office space in town for the counseling service they had dreamed about, but knew in their hearts that they were the ones who needed counseling the most. Patrick wondered how they could ever help anyone else when they needed it so much themselves. He knew that something had to change soon because it couldn't continue like it was. Either everything was going to collapse or there would be renewal of them both. Only He knew what lay ahead.

Sarah knew that she needed help outside of what she

was trying to do on her own. She had lost herself and didn't even recognize what she had become. Sarah attempted many good things in her own strength, but was running on empty. Getting the source of energy that she needed would require that she find the right filling station. Many stations were placed all around her promising to give her what she needed, but none of them gave her much mileage at all. She was realizing that she couldn't handle life anymore without help. Getting to this step was the first of a stairway that would lead to the source that she was looking for.

Sarah talked with different people trying to find someone that could help her sort things out. Susan told her about a doctor in the area that she had seen before and had helped her work through some of her own problems. After checking with some other friends that she had made since they moved, Sarah finally got enough courage to make the telephone call to get an appointment. "Hello, this is Dr. Wesley's office. How can we help you?"

"My name is Sarah Ashton. I want to get an appointment to see Dr. Wesley as a new patient sometime soon."

"Okay, Sarah. How does next Friday afternoon at 3:00 sound?"

"That will be fine. Thank you very much."

Sarah was pretty nervous about her appointment, but knew that she had to get relieved of the chains that bound her down. She had cancelled her appointments for the day so that she could spend the morning at home. It had been hard for her to get up in the mornings because she just couldn't sleep well at night. Sarah left early enough for her appointment so that she would be able to drive by the cemetery again and visit the graves of her mom, dad, and brother. She wanted so much to be able to ask them what to do about so many things, or to just tell them about her doctor's appointment that afternoon. It was as if she thought she might get some last minute revelation by going out to the cemetery and not have to keep that appointment. She arrived at Dr. Wesley's office a little early so she could get the initial paperwork done that was required for new patients.

As she got out of her car, she didn't know it as such, but her unseen enemy was there to try to discourage her from going inside. She suddenly had thoughts of every reason why she didn't need to keep that appointment. Thinking of how much time it would take, of all the other things that she needed to be doing, that her life really wasn't as bad as she thought, that the doctor probably wouldn't want to listen to her, that other people might think she was mentally ill, that she would probably feel better with a little more time, and many other thoughts flooded her mind in a concerted attempt to keep her from talking to this physician who knew the Great Physician.

CHAPTER TWENTY

Healing Begins

When Sarah had told Dr. Wesley much of her past life's history, he could easily understand why she had so many of the physical complaints she presented with. He already knew of Sarah and Patrick when they moved back into town recently, but certainly didn't know all of the trouble that Sarah had been through before. Sarah had related all of this to him over several office visits when they discussed further why she felt so depressed.

On this first visit, Dr. Wesley started Sarah on an antidepressant medication which started working within a few weeks and helped her to be able to cope again. Her problems couldn't be solved with just starting her on a medication and Dr. Wesley knew that he would only be helping the symptoms of the real problem if he took that approach only. During the follow-up visits that came every couple of weeks, he helped Sarah to explore her past and how it helped to shape her current thought patterns and outlook on life. Sarah learned that a correct knowledge of history is important if one is not going to repeat the mistakes of the past.

Unfortunately, Dr. Wesley had heard many of the same

stories from other patients. They were all a little different, but many shared a common theme of a family destroyed by various means. All of the problems that people faced started with a decision that was made in just a few seconds of time, but had consequences that lasted for years, or even generations. Dr. Wesley had seen this so many times that he knew how to help. Sarah had to break the cycle that had started with her grandparents. It was a cycle of bad decisions that led to bad relationships which caused breakdown of family structure and a repeat of the cycle over and over again with each generation. Sarah had to be healed of these hurts before the effects would be seen in her own children that she might have one day.

One of the first things that Sarah learned was that she had to be able to acknowledge the past and talk about it, which she did with Dr. Wesley. All of the hurt that she had endured caused her to develop anger that she suppressed, at the time out of necessity. She certainly couldn't express it in any way that she could figure out then. Trying to survive was the objective during those tumultuous times. The anger that she suppressed, however, had to come out in some form or another, sooner or later. Looking back, Sarah could now understand that the times of her disobedience, poor grades in school, inattentiveness, poor nutritional intake, and irritable mood were actually because of the emotions she was trying to handle on her own. Dr. Wesley helped Sarah to see that her anger had led to bitterness, and that bitterness had led to depression and/or other emotional and physical problems.

Patrick certainly noticed the change in Sarah's behavior over the couple of months that Dr. Wesley had been working with her. The circumstances that used to bother her so much didn't seem to be so concerning to her any longer. She wasn't so withdrawn now and enjoyed his presence more. Sarah even started to enjoy going to various small group gatherings at their church more often. Patrick was so glad to see Sarah getting better that he called Dr. Wesley to tell him how much better Sarah was.

On the sixth visit, Dr. Wesley brought up the issue of guilt with Sarah. She certainly understood that everyone had been given the ability to feel guilt. It is a good thing because it prompts the person to seek restitution and resolution of the problem. What is unhealthy is when someone doesn't understand or refuses to resolve guilt in the way that God intended. Dr. Wesley explained how so many people try to resolve their feelings of guilt by trying to make up for past mistakes through doing good things on their own in an attempt to balance out the scales. What they don't understand is that human means of trying to relieve guilt in this way do not work.

Sarah intellectually knew from going to church and reading her Bible that guilt had to taken away by her Creator, but she was not practically doing this. After her visit that day, Sarah prayed that God would take away her guilt through His forgiveness for her past sins. She felt relieved to truly realize the full meaning of grace—-undeserved favor. Although Sarah didn't deserve it, God had placed her in a right relationship with Him and had erased the slate clean because of Christ's sacrifice for her. Sarah finally understood that she didn't have to try to deserve this gift on her own. She knew that it was impossible to earn her salvation. It was a relief to know of a gift that would make her whole again, and it was free for the asking.

When Sarah finally understood the complete significance of how she had been given such a gift, she knew that it was her responsibility then to be gracious to others in the same way that He had been gracious to her. On the seventh visit, Dr. Wesley talked with Sarah about the topic of Chris. The abuse that Sarah had endured from Chris was what haunted her the most. Sarah could hardly fathom the possibility of what Dr. Wesley suggested to her. She couldn't face the reality of doing what she knew was the truth—-she had to forgive Chris.

When Dr. Wesley told her this, she recoiled in anger, "How can you expect me to forgive that rat for all of the harm that he caused? He murdered my mother and brother. He raped me repeatedly when I was a child, kidnapped me, and abused me so badly. And you think I should forgive him, after what he has done to me and my family? We didn't do anything to cause him to do those things to us. My mother just wanted a husband and a father for us. He took advantage of us and now look what kind of shape things are. I hope he rots in that jail he's in and society will be better off without him." Sarah started crying about half-way through her rampage and even though her words came from her heart, she knew that she could no longer continue to feel that way. Although Chris was in jail, she was in a jail, too, that she had made for herself. Sarah realized fully that the key to opening that cell door and being free was putting into practice what Christ had done for her. Still, though, she found it very difficult to even consider. Dr. Wesley prayed with Sarah that He would help her through changing her heart so that she could have the strength to do something she couldn't do on her own.

After Sarah got home, she told Patrick that night about what Dr. Wesley had said that day. Patrick told her that he agreed and that she needed to forgive Chris. It was a step for her to just be able to admit that she needed to do that. Patrick and Sarah both prayed together that night that she would be able to want to forgive Chris.

Sarah had found it easy to forgive people for minor problems or insults. Things that didn't matter too much were easier to forgive, but something like this was a bit much to ask of her, she thought. She remembered then, however, what Dr. Wesley had reminded her of right before he talked with her about forgiveness. Jesus hadn't done anything ever in His life to justify how He was treated.

Sarah knew that she was in the same boat with every other human who has been guilty of some sin in their life. Jesus forgave even the people who nailed him on the cross and He stated that they didn't know what they were doing. Sarah knew from reading in her Bible about the garden of Gethsemane that it was difficult for Jesus to go to the cross. She realized that He had made a willful decision to go that course and she had to make her mind up that she was going to follow His example. She could do it with His strength.

After a week of praying about it and asking Him to change her heart, Sarah went out to the city park at lunch one day. She found a big oak tree similar to one that she used to go sit under when she was at the university and nestled down between the wide, sturdy roots that held the old tree firmly like pillars. As she ate her lunch, she watched some kids playing out on the ball field nearby. They were having a great time with each other. As she watched, another kid, a smaller boy, came walking up from the other side of the field as several kids were gathering together, pointing, and laughing at the littler boy who kept coming their way. One of the bigger kids decided he wanted to show how tough he was so he ran up and pushed down the little boy.

Sarah was incensed at what she saw and got up to run to the defense of the little boy who seemed so weak. When Sarah got over there, the big boy suddenly had a change in demeanor as he knew that he wouldn't be able to overcome her. Sarah grabbed the big boy and held him as she asked the little boy what she should do with him. She figured that the little boy would want to come over and pound on him a few times, or do something to get the big boy back. The little boy got up and dusted his pants off. He was still a little shaken from it all, but came over and thanked Sarah for coming to his rescue. What he did next was a surprise to them all.

The little boy who had done no wrong extended his hand out to the big boy as he asked him if they could be friends.

He didn't seek the revenge that he could have and it caused the big boy to have a change of heart. Sarah let the big boy go free and he went over to the little boy to help finish dusting him off and straighten up his clothes. The big boy put his arm around the little boy's shoulder and told him he was sorry. He then invited him to come over and join their group playing on the ball field.

They all ran off together as Sarah knelt there alone to deal with this lesson played out in front of her. She knew that He was trying to help her learn. If a child could learn this valuable lesson and put it into practice even when he was given the open opportunity to take a different path, surely she could become like that child. Sarah walked back over to the tree and sat under its outstretched arms of security and protection. She prayed and thanked Him for speaking to her that day. Now she knew what she needed to do.

Sarah went home that evening and had a talk with Patrick about what her plans were. Patrick was a little nervous about it, but agreed to go with her because he could tell that she wasn't the originator of this idea. Sarah was going to go see Chris in prison. Patrick called the authorities there to be sure that Chris would be there and available to talk with Sarah. They made arrangements to be off for a week from their practice so that they could make the trip. This was going to be one of the hardest things that Sarah had ever done because she was willfully putting herself into this situation that was going to bring back a lot of bad memories, but she knew that she had to do so.

In the two weeks leading up to their scheduled trip, she saw Dr. Wesley again who was pleased with her decision. He was also pleased with how much progress she had made in becoming mentally, spiritually, and physically healthy again. After encouraging Sarah in making such a bold move, he told her that he would be praying for her, Patrick, and Chris.

CHAPTER TWENTY ONE

Becoming Whole

Before Sarah and Patrick left on their trip, Sarah took some time to sit down and reflect on all that she wanted to say to Chris. She had to express her true feelings to him. She wanted him to know how much she had been hurt all of those years. It took her quite a while to be able to put into words what she felt, but the process of doing that made her clarify in her own mind how she really did feel. Sarah knew that if she didn't take the time to write the thoughts down, she would get there and freeze up when she had a chance to speak to Chris.

Patrick asked Sarah before they left if she was sure that she wanted to do this and she smiled in the affirmative. It had been many years since that time she could never forget and she was glad that now she would be able to put the anxiety and depression to rest. Those demons that tormented her mind were about to be gone because their claim on her was being overridden. The very thought of being really free was something that could only make her happier than she'd been in a long time. Patrick and Sarah sang together while they were traveling. It was a trip to drop off some baggage and come back home without it.

When they arrived in the city where the prison was located, it was late that night. They got a hotel room which was nearby and got some much needed rest for the upcoming day. Before they retired for the night, they thanked Him for protecting them on their trip and for providing a refuge for Sarah for all of those years. Looking back, Sarah knew that He had been there not keeping her from her trials, but was there with her through them. She knew that He had led her to this point where she could be whole again and could be the kind of witness for Him that others needed. He had provided the same type of people along her way to help her and now she would provide that same help to others.

Sarah and Patrick slept well knowing that they were like two doves hidden in the cleft of the Rock together. Even with the storms of life raging around them, they could be at peace knowing that He was their refuge. Sarah, like so many others, had sought refuge in many ways. Those man-made refuges were all built on sand and crumbled with the first test of the character of the construction. She wasn't to look to the created, including man, for her healing and for a place of refuge; she was to look to Him who had made her and was the Author and Finisher of her faith.

The next morning arrived quickly and they left for the prison together. When they got there, they saw the tall fences topped with sharp, razor wire and guard posts every few hundred feet. Another tall fence was inside that fence. After they were allowed inside, they saw the huge gates shut behind them. They were glad that they were going to be allowed back out of there and wondered at how it must feel to come in knowing that it would be a long time before seeing the outside world again.

After going through numerous check points, they were allowed inside the visitation area. Patrick offered to let

Sarah meet Chris again alone, but she wanted to have him there beside her. Sarah wanted him to see that she was able to find someone who loved her the way that it was meant to be. Patrick and Sarah prayed for His strength as the guard went to get Chris.

When the guard came back, Sarah looked through the thick, sound-proof Plexiglas not knowing what she might see. She certainly expected to see the changes of aging, but what she saw was much more than that. Sarah saw a man who physically looked like the broken man that he was; he was much older looking than she expected and had a face that was hardened into a cold stare from the emptiness inside. The years that he had spent in prison had taken a great toll on him physically even though he had the facilities to exercise and wholesome meals had been provided. The mental stresses of the crimes he had committed continually wreaked havoc on him. Even other prisoners who found out what he had done didn't want to be around him. The demons that promised him pleasure and freedom had their way when Chris chose to listen all those years ago. He was now in jail with no pleasure at all. His jail was more than physical; it was spiritual, too.

Sarah sat with Patrick at her side as they escorted Chris in to sit in the chair across from them. Microphones were provided on each side so they could talk. Chris gave each of them such a mean and cold stare that it sent chills down their spines. Each of them said a silent prayer to themselves as they were face to face with evil that had consumed the man in front of them. They were speechless at first and Chris curtly said to them, "Who are you and what do you want?"

Sarah was surprised that he couldn't recognize her and it was tempting to leave after she had seen him. She had seen what he'd become and could leave knowing that he'd paid dearly for what he'd done. If she had gone there just to seek vengeance, she could feel assured that it had occurred and was continuing. “Chris, I’m Sarah and this is my husband, Patrick.”

Chris tucked his head down for a second and swallowed hard as he had been caught off guard. He quickly became defensive. “Well, what do you want from me? You see what I’ve got now. Does this make you happy to see me like this?”

“No, it doesn’t. I …,” Sarah started to say before Chris butted in.

“What do you want then? Are you here trying to get me punished more? You probably wish I’d been executed, don’t you?” Chris was getting red he was so filled with rage.

“I only wanted to come to see you face to face so I could talk to you. I want you to meet my husband, Patrick. He’s a wonderful man who has always treated me with the respect that a lady deserves.” Sarah tried to continue, but Chris broke in again.

“You want to rub it in my face, don’t you? I should have finished you off after I got what I wanted. You were such a sweet, young thing then. I wouldn’t have you now.” Chris smiled as he thought he had struck a nerve with Sarah. It did bother her hearing such insults, but she knew from the Holy Spirit’s guidance that the great accuser and the forces of darkness which controlled him would make him think anything to keep her quiet.

Patrick would have loved to have gotten Chris by the throat for saying such a thing, but controlled himself knowing that there was more than met the eye here. Thankfully, there was also a physical wall between them. This was a spiritual battle in front of his eyes that couldn’t be won by a physical struggle. Patrick prayed silently as he sat there.

“Chris, I want to tell you how I’ve felt all of these years,” Sarah tried to continue.

“Oh, so you want to come in here and make me feel guilty about it all. That’s it, isn’t it? You want to come in here and unload so you can feel better. Is that it?” Chris had gotten up and was pointing at her as his voice escalated. He couldn't understand why she really had come.

"Chris, will you please just listen, for just a few minutes?" Sarah was getting a little teary eyed.

The guard stepped in and told Sarah and Patrick, "If you want, I'll just take this scum bag back in and put him where he needs to go. He is never going to listen to you anyway." Sarah looked over at Chris in the same way that she used to when he had hurt her so many times before.

"I'll listen to what you've got to say," Chris said as he plopped back down in his chair.

Sarah got her papers that she had used to write her thoughts. She held them firmly as she read, "You took my innocence from me and made me lose my childhood. Why couldn't you have just been happy with my mother instead of hurting me so bad like you did, and then killing my mother and brother when you got caught? All of these years since then you've been in prison, but you put me in a prison the day you started abusing me. I trusted you to be the kind of father that I needed since my dad was killed by that robber, but you never intended to be that kind of person from the start. You tricked all of us into trusting you and then you took what you wanted. It's taken me years to be able to trust someone again and to really have faith in anything but myself again, but I've finally realized that I shouldn't hate you. I should have pity for you and I feel sorry for you, Chris. Chris, you don't have to finish your life like it's gone so far. I mean it when I say this: I forgive you. I really forgive you."

Chris was shaken to the core when he heard those words of forgiveness. He was shaken just like that when he turned on the radio that time while he was fleeing with Sarah tied up in the back of car. The words that he heard then made him tear the radio out of the car, but now he remembered how he should have listened to that tug on him that was prompting him to choose a different path. Now, he was ready to listen.

Miraculously, Sarah then quoted the same words that he had heard on the radio then, "*For God so loved the world that He gave His only begotten Son, that whoever believes in Him should not perish but have everlasting life. For God did not send His Son into the world to condemn the world, but that the world through Him might be saved. He who believes in Him is not condemned; but he who does not believe is condemned already, because he has not believed in the name of the only begotten Son of God. And this is the condemnation, that the light has come into the world, and men loved darkness rather than light, because their deeds were evil. For everyone practicing evil hates the light and does not come to the light, lest his deeds should be exposed. But he who does the truth comes to the light, that his deeds may be clearly seen, that they have been done in God*" (John 3:16-21).

As Sarah read those words, Chris broke down and cried like a child. Patrick sat there in amazement at what was happening in front of him. "Sarah, I'm sorry for how I hurt you. I'm sorry that I killed Julia and Frank, Jr. I shouldn't have done it. I don't know what came over me. It was like something else was controlling me. I've been tormented all of these years with the thoughts of what I did. I expected you to be coming here to condemn me further, but you came to forgive me for something that I did to you. You didn't ever deserve what I did. I'm so sorry." Chris had tears flowing like they hadn't for years. He held his head down and had a truly sorrowful spirit about him.

Sarah was crying, too, as she saw a spirit crushed in front of her just as she had been. "Chris, you don't have to live the rest of your life just being sorry. I forgave you before I came here today. I just came to let you know how I did that. Jesus helped me to be able to forgive you just as He wants to forgive you, too, if you will ask Him and really mean it."

"I want to ask," Chris stammered the words out, and then stopped, as though he thought he'd gone too far to ever even ask.

"If you believe in Him, then just ask Him; ask Jesus to forgive you for all of your sins and confess them to Him, no matter what it is." Sarah was saying words that she thought she'd never say to Chris.

"Jesus, I do believe in you. I know you tried to talk some sense into me many times before I made such a mess of my life. Then, when I did those horrible things, you still tried to talk to me through that preacher on the radio. I chose not to listen, then. But Lord, I'm ready to listen now and you sent the very one who I hurt the most to tell me again. Jesus, I've got a long list of sins to talk to you about later. You know what they are and I admit it. I'm dirty and full of the worst kind of it. I need you to forgive me and come into my life, Jesus." Chris felt what was like a rush of wind leaving him as he felt a release of the chains that bound him for so many years. He actually felt love and joy filling what was an empty void inside of him. His facial expression changed completely and was softened. He sat there crouched over for several minutes and just cried. The guard at his side couldn't help but to shed a few tears, too, as he saw true repentance in front of him.

Sarah wanted so much to be able to give him a hug as she showed Chris the same kind of love that Jesus had shown her. Not only had Chris felt a release of his own demons that controlled him for so long, but Sarah felt even a greater sense of peace after having done what He had told her she must. She was finally able to let this go and even better was the fact that Chris had been saved in the process. Even though Chris had put Him away all of those years, Jesus still had a plan for giving a choice one more time through Sarah. Sarah was in awe when Chris told her that the scripture that she read was the same scripture he heard when he was listening to the radio that time when he kidnapped her. He had a plan all along and hadn't ever given up on them. That very thought made them both love Him even more.

Sarah shared with Chris for a few more minutes before they had to part ways. She told him how that now he'd been forgiven, he needed to totally surrender his life over to Jesus for the rest of his life and ask Him to sanctify him and cleanse him from his sinful nature. Sarah told Chris before they left that she would write him intermittently.

Patrick, too, tried to reassure Chris and let him know that he had made a commitment to the Lord that nobody could take from him. Patrick knew that the devil would come and tell Chris that he hadn't really meant what he said, that he was just caught up in some emotions, and that it wasn't real. Chris told Patrick that he was going to make it, with God's help, and asked Patrick and Sarah to pray for him as the guard escorted him back to his cell. As Chris went back to his cell, he knew that he had to pay the price on earth for what he had done, but that would be the end of it. His eternal sentence that was hanging over him was erased.

Sarah and Patrick left there in almost unbelief as to what had happened. Sarah asked Patrick if she really said what she thought she had said. She knew that He had spoken through her. Neither of them had had a happier moment in their lives. Their faith had grown and now someone else had found the faith that was needed. They drove back to the hotel like they were riding on a cloud. Such a feeling of peace surrounded them that they wanted to never feel another way. It was truly a mountain top experience.

As they packed their bags to head back home, they knew that after this mountain another valley would be up ahead. The difference now was that they knew, to a greater degree, Who was in control if they would just let Him lead. The journey could get rough again, but with Him being the Master, they had no fear of what lay ahead. They headed out with a greater freedom than they had ever had. They never thought before that they would be coming to let Chris out of jail, but that was exactly what He had spiritually done through them.

Going back home was like going to start over again with a newness and freshness about everything around them. After Sarah got back home, she saw Dr. Wesley the next week. He was elated at what had taken place and actually cried himself as Sarah related what happened. Dr. Wesley saw such a change in Sarah that he recommended that she cut her antidepressant medication in half for the next month, and then she was able to quit taking it. She found out that she didn't need it anymore, as the Lord had healed her and had made her whole again. By two months from then, Dr. Wesley told her that he only needed to see her if something new came up and otherwise she could come in for once a year check-ups.

Patrick and Sarah both enjoyed each other more than they ever had before. The work that they did was filled with expectancy at what He might have planned for them, if they just remained sensitive to His leading. Their practice was a place of healing for many people over the years ahead.

Sarah had a child a year later and named him Samuel. Patrick and Sarah had dedicated him to the Lord before he was even conceived. They prayed for him to come to know Him like them and serve the Lord all of his life in the manner that He wanted. Their next child eighteen months later was named Hannah, and then a third came in another eighteen months who they named Chris. Chris later confessed what he did to his first wife before Julia. His was sentenced to another life term and knew that he would never see the freedom again on this earth. Sarah kept in touch with Chris over the years and they actually became friends enough that Patrick and Sarah would go and visit him once a year to see how he was coming along. Chris' life had truly changed and he even brought other prisoners to the Lord over the years ahead.

Sarah, Patrick, and many others learned and lived what Christ demanded of those who follow him. They knew that He didn't desire sacrifice, He wanted obedience first. The cycle had been broken in many lives because of the obedience of one person who then could impact others. The One Who gets the credit, although, was the One Who was obedient unto death, even death upon the cross—Jesus Christ.

Jeremiah 29

plans to prosper you

& Not harm you.

John 3:16

one and only Son

saves the world.

Printed in the United States
21385LVS00003B/85-1008